FASHION VICTIM

'I think,' said Charlie, taking off her round, wire-rimmed glasses and polishing them on her scarf, 'that maybe we need to try and keep our ideas for this fashion show a bit more simple. Your design's really nice, Jas, but it's just too ambitious.'

'Exactly,' agreed Liz. 'We've got to be more realistic.'

Jas felt hurt. Now she was under attack from her own friends. 'Your outfits can be as realistic as you want,' she protested hotly, 'but I want to have a go at making this.' She held her chin defiantly in the air.

Liz looked pained 'Jas, it's supposed to be fun. Where's the fun if you have to stay at home night after night, sewing?'

'They're right,' Becky said nodding. 'I think you're taking this whole competition too seriously.'

Jas wasn't sure if she wanted to shout at them or burst into tears. How could her best friends treat her this way?

Fashion Victim
Bell Street 4

Holly Tate

Knight Books
Hodder and Stoughton

Copyright © 1993 by Complete Editions Ltd

First published in Great Britain 1993 by Knight Books,
a division of Hodder Headline PLC.

The right of Holly Tate to be identified as the author of
the Work has been asserted by her in accordance with the
Copyright, Designs and Patents Act 1988.

10 9 8 7 6 5 4 3 2 1

ISBN 0 340 58229 4

Printed and bound in Great Britain by
Cox & Wyman Ltd, Reading, Berkshire

Hodder and Stoughton Children's Books
A Division of Hodder Headline PLC
47 Bedford Square
London WC1B 3DP

1

'I'm soaked!' groaned Jasmine Scott as she squelched into 2K's form room. A trickle of water dripped from her short dark hair and down the back of her neck.

Becky Burns, who was already sitting at her desk, viewed her friend in horror. 'Why didn't you wear a raincoat or bring an umbrella?' she asked, combing out her blonde hair.

'I couldn't find an umbrella,' Jas grumbled in her husky voice, pulling her games kit towel out from her backpack. 'And I hate raincoats: they're so uncool. Anyway, my mum was supposed to give me a lift. I only asked her to wait two minutes till I was ready, but when I came downstairs she'd gone. Why do parents have to be so impatient?'

'Pass.' Becky smiled. 'My dad's just the same. No time to wait.'

'Hey, look at Gina,' Jas said quickly. 'See what I mean about raincoats?' Jas pointed at Gina Galloway, who was pushing her way up the crowded aisle to her seat at the back of the class.

Becky giggled. Gina's silver plastic trenchcoat must have cost a fortune; otherwise she wouldn't be wearing it. Gina was the snobbiest girl in the class and she never wore anything ordinary. But with her fluffy lemon-coloured hair and white face, the raincoat made her look like an alien from outer space.

Jas started towelling her hair. It was so short that it would only take a few minutes to dry completely. Then she straightened up and took a look at her black wool jacket.

'I think this is ruined, you know. It's supposed to be dry-cleaned, not soaked.'

'Why don't you put it on a radiator?' suggested Becky.

'Good idea,' Jas nodded, peeling the jacket off and finding space for it on the radiator between Jamie Thompson's navy sweatshirt and a pair of grey socks. 'Whose socks?' she asked suspiciously.

'Ryan Bryson's,' Becky warned, 'so don't get too near them or the smell might kill you!'

'Yuck, pass the gas masks!' Jas held her nose and sat down again just as Miss Tyler came in.

Even Miss Tyler looked damp this morning. Her hair curled round her face and her scarlet jacket had rain spots across the shoulders.

'This place is more like a laundry than a class-room,' she commented cheerfully, looking at all the wet clothing laid out to dry. 'Into your seats everyone, please. We've got a lot to get through before the first lesson.'

There were groans as the class settled down. 'My trousers are soaked,' complained Ryan Bryson.

'Take them off and put them on the radiator,' someone told him.

The rest of the class squealed in protest. 'Don't let him do it, Miss!' called Mina Chotai.

Miss Tyler cast Ryan a shrewd glance over the top of her red glasses. 'Keep your trousers on, Ryan,' she warned. 'But as we're on the subject of clothes, I have some news that may interest the fashion fans among you.' She took a folder from her bag.

Jas perked up. Anything to do with fashion interested her.

Miss Tyler didn't look so enthusiastic though. She pursed her lips, shiny with bright red lipstick, as she glanced at the folder. 'This is really most annoying. We should have had all this information several weeks ago, so that we could plan things properly,' she said, shaking her head. 'Have you all seen a programme on TV called *Threads*?'

The class was a sea of nodding heads. Jas turned excitedly to Becky, her chocolate-coloured eyes glowing. 'It's that fashion programme,' said Becky, chewing one of her fingernails in excitement.

'I know!' Jas replied, feeling a bit indignant. After all, wasn't she the fashion expert in their gang? Didn't she read every fashion magazine she could lay her hands on? And didn't she *always* watch *Threads*?

'*Threads* is holding a competition to find the young designer of the year,' Miss Tyler continued. 'To enter, students must divide themselves into teams of four and make outfits based on a theme.'

Jas could hardly contain herself. 'What's the theme, Miss Tyler?' she called out.

'Holidays,' Miss Tyler replied. 'They're looking for outfits with a holiday theme.' She tapped her red pencil on the desk in annoyance. 'It would have been nice to turn the competition into a school project and develop your ideas in the Fashion and Textiles class, but there isn't going to be time. Mr Leach has asked me to organise a fashion show to

7

display the outfits on the Friday after next. It's not long enough, but that is the only date available – which means the teams will have about two weeks to design and make the clothes.'

The class buzzed with chatter as she took a piece of chalk and wrote the details of the competition on the board in big, spiky writing – the sort she used when she was in a bad mood.

'Do you get the feeling Miss Tyler isn't too thrilled about this competition?' Becky asked, giggling.

'I don't know why,' Jas said, writing down the details in her organiser. 'I think it sounds great.'

'What happens to the winning team?' Gina asked. Usually she had a really bored tone of voice, but for once she sounded interested.

'The winner from this school goes through to the next round, which will be the regional final. The winners of that will appear on *Threads*, and one of the regional contestants will be chosen as Young Designer of the Year,' Miss Tyler explained.

'Just imagine it,' Jas said with a sigh. 'Wouldn't it be brilliant? Millions of people seeing your designs on TV . . .'

'Yeah,' agreed Becky. Then she frowned. 'I just wish we had a bit more time.'

But Jas wasn't listening. Her eyes shone with excitement. She'd always wanted to work in fashion, and here was her big chance to make a name for herself. It was perfect. She could just imagine the scene now. The lights and cameras of the TV show, models wearing the beautiful outfits she'd created, and a voice announcing, *'Ladies and gentlemen, please meet the Young Designer of the Year – Jasmine Scott!'*

Her heart began to race at the thought of it. It was her dream come true. More than anything, she wanted to win that title. But she was going to have to work fast to do it!

'You'll be in our team, won't you?' Liz Newman put her arm round Jas's damp shoulders as they went down the corridor to their chemistry lesson.

'Of course she will,' said Becky, bouncing along on the other side. Charlie Farrell fell into step beside them.

'Or maybe she can think of a better team to join,' Charlie added jokily, shaking her long red hair.

'Don't be silly,' Jas protested. The four of them always did things together. 'We'll be the best team in the school, no problem. The others don't stand a chance against us.'

'Yeah!' Becky punched the air.

'Why don't you come round to my place after school?' Jas suggested. 'We can design our outfits and make a list of the things we'll need to buy for them. There's not much time – we've got to start as soon as possible.'

'I can't come,' Charlie said with an apologetic shrug. 'I've already said I'll go over to the animal shelter to help out there.' She twisted a strand of her long hair and began plaiting it.

'Can't you get out of it, just this once?' Jas asked.

'No, I promised Helen, the woman who runs the shelter, I'd go – and I keep my promises.'

'Please?' Jas pouted pleadingly. 'I'm sure she'd understand if she knew how important it was.'

'No!' Charlie said vehemently. 'I don't just go

9

round there stroking fluffy kittens, you know. It's hard work. The other day someone brought in a dog that had been really badly beaten. It wouldn't let anyone touch it, so Helen's given me the task of getting its trust back – and that means going round there regularly to see it.'

'Poor thing,' said Becky, shaking her head. 'I don't know how anyone can treat animals like that.'

'Well, lots of people do,' growled Charlie. 'Including some people at this school.'

'Who?' Jas asked.

'Let's just say I've got my suspicions,' said Charlie.

Liz was looking uncomfortable. 'I'm sorry, Jas, but you'll have to count me out as well. I've promised my mum I'll babysit for Holly straight after school.'

Jas felt her smile begin to fade a bit. Then she had an idea. 'Maybe Becky and I could come round to your place instead?' she suggested brightly. 'We could help you with the babysitting and talk about our ideas at the same time.'

But Becky stopped her. 'Actually, Jas, I can't make it tonight. I told Daniel I'd see him.' Daniel Armstrong was Becky's boyfriend.

'Daniel wouldn't mind if you changed your plans, would he?' Jas said. 'You could always see him some other time.'

Becky looked at her as if she'd said something crazy. 'But I promised Daniel I'd see him,' she said indignantly.

It didn't seem like a good enough excuse to Jas. After all, Becky could see Daniel any night of the week. 'He'd understand why you needed to work on the competition tonight, wouldn't he?' she persisted.

Becky wrinkled her nose and glanced at the other two. 'But I want to see him. And if you really want to know, I'm not that excited at having to sew an outfit for the fashion show. Sewing is so boring!'

Jas couldn't believe her ears. How did Becky expect to design and model an outfit without sewing it, too? Liz must have seen the storm brewing on Jas's face, because she tried to calm things down.

'There's no need for us to start work right away, is there?' she said as the lab door opened and Mr Harris asked them to go in. 'There's always tomorrow. And we can give Becky a hand with the sewing if she needs it.'

Liz's advice was sensible, as usual, but Jas still felt disappointed. What had got into her friends? One minute they'd been eager to take part in the competition and now they were making excuses to get out of it.

Why couldn't her friends see that this was the opportunity of a lifetime? Was she the only one who was taking the competition seriously?

Jas walked home from school with her head down, thinking. It had stopped raining at last and the sun was drying up the puddles on the pavement.

There was nothing to prevent her from starting work on the design for her own outfit, even if her friends weren't available, she decided. She could start work this evening – and maybe when they saw her designs, they'd be more enthusiastic.

The Scott family lived in a modern house on one of Wetherton's new estates. Until two years ago they'd lived in a smaller place in the same street as Liz Newman. Then Mrs Scott's career as a marketing executive had taken off and Jas's parents had decided to move somewhere bigger. Jas liked the house, though she sometimes missed having her old friends just down the road.

As she walked up the drive, she remembered that today was Tuesday, and that made her feel even better. On Tuesdays her big sister, Abby, came home from college early.

If there was one thing Abby loved, it was clothes and fashion. She'd always bought fashion magazines and fussed about what she wore, and Jas had learned a lot from her. Last year, when they'd been at school together, Jas had felt so proud of having an older sister around. Not just because of the way she dressed, but because she was popular and fun, too. She wasn't stand-offish, either, like some people's older brothers and sisters, and she didn't treat Jas and her friends like idiots. Everyone liked Abby.

'I wish I had a big sister like her,' Liz had said one evening when Abby had taken them out bowling. Jas had felt really proud and lucky.

And of course, having Abby around meant that Jas could borrow clothes from her. Though recently, she had to admit, it hadn't been worth raiding Abby's wardrobe. There was never anything new.

Since Abby had started college, where she was training to be a nursery nurse, she'd changed. She seemed to have grown up a lot. Before, Jas had felt really close to her, but now her sister seemed more and more like a stranger. They didn't go out shopping together as they used to. They'd often gone out on Friday nights, too, bowling or ice-skating or maybe to see a film.

But they didn't do that any more. And Abby had stopped wearing her really fashionable clothes. Most of the time she just wore jeans, because they were more practical for crawling around on the floor with little kids.

'Anyway, none of the students at college have got any money for clothes,' she had said. 'We all just wear jeans and our old gear. It's not cool to be too flash.'

Maybe this competition would get Abby interested in fashion again, Jas thought, approaching the house and searching in her backpack for the front door keys. Perhaps it would be a chance for them to get close again – like they had been. She hoped so.

Jas could hear the TV as she opened the door. That meant Abby was home. Jas threw her bag and jacket down in the hall and hurried into the sitting room. She could see a pair of feet sticking up from one end of the sofa.

'Abby, wait till you hear what's happened,' Jas exclaimed, leaning over the back of the sofa and tugging at the feet. Then she stopped dead. 'Oh!'

Her sister was stretched out on the cushions – and so was her boyfriend, Stuart. It was his feet Jas had tugged. And judging from the furious look on Abby's face, Jas got the feeling that she'd interrupted some serious smooching.

'Whoops,' she muttered, letting go of Stuart's toes.

'Do you have to come barging in like that?' Abby

demanded, sitting up and darting a poisonous look at Jas. She had long, curly dark hair and eyes just like Jas's – two chocolate buttons surrounded by long black lashes.

'I'm sorry,' said Jas, noticing that her sister was blushing. 'What were you doing?' she teased.

'Nothing!' Abby growled, looking as if she was about to explode. 'Go away, little sister.'

'Why don't you go and do nothing in your room?' Jas said cheekily.

'You know very well that Stuart's not allowed in my room,' Abby replied. 'Now get lost, Jas.'

Stuart sat up and smoothed back his hair. 'Hi,' he said with a sigh that made Jas feel like an intruder in her own home. 'What's all the fuss about?'

When Abby first came home from college and announced that she was going out with a photography student, Jas had felt really excited. She imagined a gorgeous hunk of a guy, maybe a bit like her pop idol Rory Todd, with dark glasses and a camera. She could just see him photographing beautiful models for glossy magazines, or taking pictures of film stars and hit bands. The way Abby talked about him, he was the most amazing person in the world.

One day, Abby brought Stuart home. And that was the end of all Jas's dreams, because Stuart was just – well, ordinary. He wasn't tall, dark and handsome. In fact he was only a couple of inches taller than Abby, and he had a spot on his chin. His hair was a gingery colour and he wore pink Bermuda shorts that made his legs look weedy.

Jas had been amazed that Abby, who was normally so fussy about her clothes and boyfriends, would even think of going out with him. Nothing about Stuart lived up to Jas's expectations.

Not even his photos. They were all black and white shots of boring landscapes, or arty pictures of old ladies sitting on windswept beaches. As far as Jas was concerned, Stuart was a total let-down.

But Abby didn't think so. When Jas tried to point out how ordinary he was, Abby wouldn't hear a word of it.

'You're too young to appreciate him,' she said. 'Stuart and I really like each other for what we are, not how we look. With him I can be myself. I don't have to dress up or pretend anything. He makes me feel really special – just for being me.'

Her eyes went all gooey as she said it. She was always going on about him, how special he was, how interesting the places he took her to were . . . It seemed Stuart could do no wrong.

And Jas was sick of it. Before Stuart came along, she and Abby had hung around together a lot. Friday evenings had been *their* time. But now Abby never had time for anything or anyone except Stuart and her college course, and Jas felt left out.

Stuart wasn't very interested in fashion, so Abby didn't worry about what she wore any more. She didn't want to spend hours shopping for clothes, which Jas loved. She didn't even want to lie around listening to tapes or to practice dancing. As far as Jas was concerned, her big sister had got serious and boring – and there was only one person to blame: Stuart Conroy.

It was all his fault. If it wasn't for him, everything would be just as it always had been. She hated him

15

for taking Abby's attention. And it just made it worse that he was nice to Jas. If he'd been horrible, somehow it would all have been easier. But whenever he met her Stuart was always asking questions and taking an interest. Jas just wished he'd leave her alone. Or, better still, disappear entirely.

'Come on, tell us your news,' he prompted, putting his arm around Abby and giving Jas an encouraging smile.

'It doesn't matter.' Jas turned away. 'You wouldn't be interested.'

'Why not?' Stuart sounded surprised.

'It's nothing to do with you.' Jas folded her arms. 'I wanted to talk to Abby.'

'Jas!' Abby snapped. 'Why are you always so off-hand with Stuart? He only wants to know what you were looking so pleased about.'

'I don't have to tell him,' Jas shot back angrily.

'All right,' Stuart said mildly. 'Forget I asked. It's no big deal.'

Abby turned her disapproval on him. 'No, don't let her off the hook. I'm sick of her being so rude when you're around.'

Stuart shrugged at Jas. 'Looks as if we're both in trouble now!' he said with a laugh.

Jas kept her face straight. He couldn't get round her by being nice. 'I wanted to tell you about the *Threads* competition for the Young Designer of the Year,' she started.

'Sounds interesting,' said Stuart after Jas had finished explaining. '*Threads* is a good show. It would be brilliant publicity to have your design featured on the programme. How do you enter the competition?'

His interest irritated Jas all the more. 'There's going to be a school fashion show,' she explained grudgingly, going over the details.

Abby got up from the sofa without saying anything. 'Don't you want to hear about it?' Jas felt hurt by her sister's reaction.

'Sure. I can hear you from the kitchen. I'm going to go and make something to eat.' Abby stretched like a lazy cat. 'Though I must admit that I've got more important things than fashion competitions to worry about. Things like exams and assignments. And you,' she murmured, gazing at Stuart with a soppy look on her face.

'Well, I'm interested, even if Abby's too busy,' said Stuart, turning back to Jas.

'What?' Jas felt a bit sick. She didn't want *Stuart* to start getting enthusiastic about the competition. She hated Stuart!

'I'd like to photograph the fashion show,' he said. 'With a bit of luck I can get a photo in the local paper. And maybe, if one of the Bell Street designs wins the competition, my picture'll be in all the papers.'

'That's a great idea,' Abby called from the kitchen. 'Do you want a burger, Jas?'

'Yes!' Jas called back.

'Who should I go and talk to at the school about taking photos?' Stuart asked.

'Miss Tyler's organising the fashion show,' Jas mumbled. The last thing she wanted was Stuart turning up at school. He'd already invaded her life at home. She didn't want him worming his way into her school life, too.

17

'But she's in a really bad mood about it,' Jas warned. 'She might not want a photographer there.'

But Stuart was undeterred. 'I'll come into school and see her,' he said with the kind of enthusiasm that made Jas want to die. Things were going from bad to terrible.

After a few minutes Jas escaped to the kitchen where Abby was grilling the burgers. 'If you were asked to design an outfit with a holiday theme,' Jas said casually as she took clean plates from the dishwasher, 'what kind of thing would you do?'

'I don't know. It depends what the judges are looking for. I mean, do they want something practical, that lots of people would want to wear? Or something really creative but not necessarily commercial?' Abby shrugged. 'Just do something you really like. That's my best advice.' She sliced the buns and put a layer of lettuce in each.

'I was just hoping for a few ideas,' Jas said with a twinkle in her eyes.

Abby turned the burgers under the grill. 'I don't know what I'd do if I was entering the competition. I suppose when people go on holiday they like to lie on the beach and swim in the sea. Sea and sand. There's an idea to start you off.'

'Gee, thanks,' Jas said ironically. 'I would never have thought of that on my own!'

The phone rang. 'Probably Mum calling to say she's going to be late,' muttered Abby, rushing off to answer it. 'Finish off the burgers, will you? Stuart has barbecue sauce on his.'

Jas opened the cupboard in which all the sauces and relishes were kept. There was tomato sauce and

18

soy sauce and Mrs Scott's favourite mustard. Yellow sweetcorn relish, mint jelly, a jar of chutney, some lime pickle . . . Jas's gaze fell on the little bottle of chilli sauce her dad liked. It was super-hot. When he used it, he was careful to measure out just a few drops.

Jas couldn't resist the temptation. Stuart could do with a bit of spicing up, she thought as she flipped his burger from under the grill. He just didn't seem to take her hints that she didn't like him around. Maybe this would show him how she felt!

She covered the burger with a big spoonful of the chilli sauce, then added a blob of barbecue sauce on top. 'Here you are,' she said sweetly as she took it through to the sitting room, where he was watching TV.

'Thanks.' He smiled as he took the plate from her. Jas scampered back to the kitchen and waited for the screams. They didn't take long.

'Water!' Stuart yelled, staggering into the kitchen, clutching his throat. His face was bright red and Jas could almost see steam coming out of his ears.

Stifling a satisfied smile, she reached for a small glass, filled it from the tap and passed it to him. 'Thirsty?' she asked innocently. Stuart swigged it and gasped.

'More!' He pushed her aside in his rush to get to the sink.

'What's going on?' demanded Abby, coming through the door. 'Stuart, what's wrong?'

'My throat's on fire!' he muttered, between gulps of water.

'What's going on?' Abby asked. She looked round

– and before Jas could conceal it, saw the bottle of chilli sauce sitting on the worktop. Jas kicked herself. Why hadn't she put it away before giving Stuart the burger?

'It was a joke,' Jas insisted, backing away from her sister. 'I thought Stuart might like something a bit spicier than barbecue sauce.'

'I don't believe a word of it!' Abby wagged her finger close to Jas's nose, her dark curls bobbing up and down with fury. 'That was a mean thing to do!'

Jas couldn't deny it – but she didn't really care, either. In fact, watching Stuart gulping and coughing made her want to laugh. 'If you can't take a joke, I won't do it again,' she said, turning away. But Abby's hand snaked out and grabbed her by the arm.

'Grow up, Jas,' she hissed. 'There are three-year-old children at the nursery who behave in a more adult way than you. I'm going to tell Mum and Dad what you've done.'

'If you do,' Jas retorted triumphantly, 'I'll tell them I caught you smooching on the sofa. They won't like that. You're not a good influence on me.'

'You're a brat, Jas!' Abby stood there almost lost for words. Almost – but not quite. 'How am I supposed to bring Stuart home when you treat him like this?'

'That's your problem,' said Jas, turning away with an unconcerned shrug of her shoulders. She slid her slightly burnt burger into its bun and then, with Abby still glaring at her, carried it upstairs to her room.

If Stuart never came to the house again, that would suit her fine, Jas thought rebelliously as she sat munching. At least now he knew he wasn't welcome here. Perhaps it wasn't enough to split him and Abby up – but Jas could hope, couldn't she?

2

Liz and Becky were hanging around at the gang's favourite spot – the grassy slope that ran from the playground down to the sports field – when Jas arrived at school the next day. After yesterday's storm it was too damp to sit down, so Becky was leaning against one of the trees.

'Hi,' Jas called excitedly as she strolled over to them. 'Wait till you see what I started yesterday evening.' She unzipped her backpack and pulled out a sketchpad. 'See . . .' Her voice trailed off. Neither of her friends had taken any notice of her!

'Oh, hi, Jas,' Liz said vaguely, tuning back in to what Becky was saying.

Jas stood there chewing her gum and feeling ignored, as Becky ran through the details of the video she and Daniel had watched last night. Liz kept nodding. 'It sounds great,' she said. 'Maybe Josh and I can rent it at the weekend.'

Boyfriends, boyfriends, boyfriends! Jas fumed silently. That was all *anyone* talked about these days. If it wasn't Abby going on and on about Stuart, it was Becky singing Daniel's praises or Liz saying how wonderful Josh was. Jas thought it was boring – particularly when there were other, more exciting things to discuss.

'Hi,' said Charlie, loping up in her usual hippy-style gear. She had a filmy orange scarf draped round her neck and a big pink rose tucked through the top buttonhole of her white shirt.

She glanced at the sketchpad. 'Have you started your design for the fashion show?'

'Started?' Jas laughed. 'I think I've finished it.' She held out the pad.

'Let's have a look,' chorused Liz and Becky, suddenly turning their attention to her. They crowded round.

Jas's picture showed a fashionable sleeveless top, fitted round the shoulders and then flaring out at the hips. Jas had made it a sandy gold colour, and round the bottom were blue frills that looked like waves. The fabric was patterned with a splashy design of shells and starfish.

'What are these?' asked Becky, pointing to a number of little blobs dotted round the neck.

'They're real shells,' Jas explained brightly. 'I thought I could sew them or stick them on. I'd like to have them scattered all over, really. And I might experiment with making some seaweed fronds out of fabric and seeing how they look round the neck.' There was ominous silence from the others. 'I did think about putting a mermaid on it somewhere, too,' Jas finished.

'How are you going to find fabric with a pattern of shells and fish like that?' Liz asked, looking concerned.

'I'm going to paint them on myself.' Jas had thought it all through last night, as she'd sat in her room and kept well out of Abby's way. 'You can paint on fabric just like you can on paper. You have to use special paints, but—'

'Or you could silk-screen a design,' mused Charlie, who was good at arty things. 'I think it's great, Jas. Really wacky. And it's given me some ideas.'

'You couldn't wear it every day, though, could you?' Liz sounded dubious. 'What would people say if you wore a top like that to school?' She smoothed back her silky hair under her velvet headband, as if to say *she'd* never wear a top like that.

Jas felt a bit ruffled. 'But it's supposed to be for a fashion show, Liz! To catch the judges' eyes we've got to make something unusual – not the kind of thing you can buy in the shops already.'

'I suppose so.' But Liz didn't look convinced.

Becky was frowning too. 'It's going to take ages to make, isn't it?' she said. 'First of all you've got to make the top—'

'But it's a really simple basic design,' Jas interrupted. 'I've already got a black top like it at home. I'm going to copy the basic shape from that.'

'Maybe,' admitted Becky, chewing on one of her fingernails as she spoke, 'but once you've made it you've got to paint the design and sew on the ruffles and stick on the shells. It's going to take years!'

'I don't mind spending time on it,' Jas said. 'You don't have to make your outfit so complicated if you don't want to.'

'And it'll be expensive,' Charlie chimed in, suddenly looking less than enthusiastic. 'It's a great idea, Jas, but by the time you've bought fabric and paints and shells—'

Jas shook her head. 'I've got a big jar of shells at

24

home. I always collect them when I go to the seaside. Seeing them gave me the idea in the first place.'

Before anyone could voice more objections, a trainer came flying over Liz's head and hit Becky on the shoulder. Vale Dixon, one of the third-year girls, raced over to get it. She was red-faced and giggling.

'Can I have it back?' she asked.

Becky had picked it up. She rubbed her shoulder. 'That hurt!'

'Sorry,' said Vale. 'I didn't mean it to hit you. I was throwing it to Vanessa.'

'Whose trainer is it, anyway?' Liz asked.

'Josie Watkins'.' While Vale was talking, she was also staring at Jas's sketch. 'She kept boasting about them, so we stole them to teach her a lesson. Here she comes now. You're not going to give it to her, are you?'

'Of course I am,' said Becky, spotting a sulky girl with long brown hair heading straight towards them. 'Here, Josie, have your trainer back.'

'Thanks.' Josie took it and turned quickly away, stuffing the trainer into her bag. 'I'll get you later, Vale,' she muttered.

Vale didn't look too concerned. 'When did you turn into such a saint, Becky?' she asked jokingly. Her eyes returned to Jas's sketchpad. 'Is this going to be your design for the fashion show?'

'What if it is?' asked Jas, covering up the pad. 'Are you snooping on the competition, Vale?'

Vale sniffed. 'Just interested, that's all. But if you've only got one pretty boring design, it's not going to get you very far, is it?'

'We've got loads of ideas,' said Charlie.

'That's okay then.' Vale turned and walked off. Her tone made it clear that she really didn't believe Charlie.

'I don't like Vale,' said Becky, her blue eyes glittering. 'Who does she think she is?'

'She's not so bad. Ignore her,' advised Liz.

But Becky still didn't look happy. And Jas felt annoyed at Vale calling her design boring, too. She knew it wasn't true. Vale said things like that out of spite, to hurt other people. The four friends stood quietly for a while.

'I think,' said Charlie at last, taking off her round, wire-rimmed glasses and polishing them on her scarf, 'that maybe we need to try and keep our ideas for this fashion show a bit more simple. Your design's really nice, Jas, but it's just too ambitious.'

'Exactly,' agreed Liz. 'We've got to be more realistic.'

Jas felt hurt. Now she was under attack from her own friends. 'Your outfits can be as realistic as you want,' she protested hotly, 'but I want to have a go at making this.' She held her chin defiantly in the air.

Liz looked pained. 'Jas, it's supposed to be fun. Where's the fun if you have to stay at home night after night, sewing?'

'They're right,' Becky said nodding. 'Don't get so carried away with it! I think you're taking this whole competition too seriously.'

Jas wasn't sure if she wanted to shout at them or burst into tears. How could her best friends treat her this way? She felt totally let down.

'If that's how you feel,' she said with quiet determination, 'I'll leave you guys to have fun on your own – because I'm going to make this outfit for the fashion show and I don't care what you do.' She stuffed her sketchpad into her backpack.

'Jas, we didn't mean it like that,' Liz tried. 'We're just saying . . .'

But Jas didn't want to hang around to hear more reasons why her ideas were no good. She stalked off across the playground.

'Had a row with your friends?' Vale Dixon came bounding up beside her.

'Just leave me alone,' Jas snapped, turning to look in the other direction. At the moment she didn't feel like talking to anyone – certainly not Vale.

'You're very prickly,' Vale observed. Jas sat down on the gym steps – and Vale plonked herself down too. She sounded quite cheerful. 'What did you fight about? That sketch you were all looking at?'

'It's nothing to do with you!' Jas protested, with a glance at Vale. She had bright red cheeks and brown hair in a short wedge cut that Jas couldn't help admiring because it was so precise – and expensive looking.

Jas didn't normally have much to do with Vale and her crowd. For a start, Vale was a year older. And she was also one of Gina Galloway's cronies. In fact Gina and Vale were nextdoor neighbours. They both lived in big houses in the poshest street in Wetherton. Vale wasn't quite as snobby as Gina, but she ran her a close second.

'*I* thought your design looked good,' announced Vale, taking Jas by surprise.

'You said it was boring!' Jas shot back, without thinking.

'Well, I didn't want to give that lot any encouragement,' Vale said, looking pleased with herself. 'But it's a pity the others in your team don't appreciate a good idea when they see it.'

'They keep saying it's too ambitious,' Jas muttered. She felt a bit disloyal, talking about the others to an outsider. But she needed to tell someone about how badly she'd been treated – and Vale did seem sympathetic. 'Liz thinks it's going to take too long to make and Charlie thinks it's too expensive.'

Vale shrugged. 'They're stupid. You have to invest a bit of time and money if you want a really good result, don't you?'

Jas nodded. Vale was right. Did Charlie really expect to make a brilliant outfit without spending any money?

'Gina's mum's promised her she can have anything she needs for her outfit,' Vale said. 'And Gina's got one of those turbo-charged sewing machines with all the latest electronic gadgets. Gina says you just have to show the machine your design and it practically sews it itself!'

'Good for Gina,' Jas said sarcastically. Trust Gina Galloway to have all the advantages. Jas took another glance at Vale. There was a strange gleam in her eye that made her suspect that Vale was leading up to something. It was like a cat and mouse game – and Jas felt like the mouse.

'It's good for me, too, because I'm in Gina's team,' Vale smiled. 'She says money's no object when it comes to winning. Not like your team.'

Jas gritted her teeth. So that was what this conversation was all about. Vale was here to boast. Well, she wasn't going to get away with it.

'What a pity that all Gina's money's going to be wasted, because without some good ideas and talent, you haven't got a hope of winning the contest.' And she picked up her backpack and walked off, leaving Vale sitting there with a surprised expression.

Even so, Jas felt rattled by what Vale had said. With Liz and Charlie and Becky so short of enthusiasm, and Gina with all the advantages, what real hope did Jas have of being in the winning team?

'Can I help you?' asked the assistant in the fabric department of Peabody's, the big department store in Wetherton's shopping mall.

'I'm just looking,' Jas sighed, gazing along the racks full of rolls of fabric. There was almost any colour and pattern you could think of. Spots and stripes, flowery designs, tartans and abstract splodges in red, yellow, blue, green and a hundred shades in between. But nothing in the sandy-gold colour she was looking for.

There was only one roll that was anywhere close, and that was more like mud than sand. Jas picked it up reluctantly. It would have to do, even if it wasn't perfect. She checked the price ticket. It was more expensive than she'd anticipated. But she wouldn't need very much, she reassured herself. A metre and a half should be okay. Or even, she thought, just one metre. The fabric was wide; she didn't want to buy too much and have to waste anything.

'One metre, please,' she told the assistant.

At another counter there was a display of fabric paints and dyes. Jas looked along the rows, searching for the colours she wanted. Gold and turquoise and pink and silver . . . She picked out the paints, feeling her excitement flooding back. It wouldn't matter about the colour of the fabric if she could decorate it beautifully.

The girl at the cash register added up the cost of the paints. 'Sixteen pounds, eighty pence,' she announced.

'What?' Jas couldn't believe it. 'They can't be that much!'

The girl looked at her as if Jas was wasting her time. 'Do you want them or not?' she asked grumpily.

Jas checked in her purse. She didn't have nearly that amount. 'I didn't realise they were so expensive. I'd better leave it,' she mumbled, feeling silly.

The woman queuing behind Jas sighed long-sufferingly. 'Sorry,' Jas muttered, trying not to cringe with embarrassment as she walked away.

Why did everything have to be so difficult? Didn't she deserve just one good break – one piece of luck or even just a few words of encouragement to help her with the fashion show?

The phone was ringing as Jas let herself into the house. 'Hi, Jas,' said Stuart in his usual friendly voice when she answered. He seemed to have forgotten yesterday and the chilli-burger, which disappointed Jas.

'How's your throat?' she asked, reminding him.

'Much better,' he said with a laugh. 'That was great trick you pulled!'

Jas couldn't believe it. She'd thought the chilli would put him off, but instead he seemed to think it was just some kind of a joke. What would she have to do to make him realise he wasn't wanted around here? Put poison in his coffee?

'Could you tell Abby that I'll meet her outside the cinema at seven o'clock?' he asked. 'I said I'd meet her in the cafe at six, but I'm going to be late.'

'Right,' said Jas matter-of-factly. 'Is that it?'

'That's all.' Stuart still sounded amused, which just wound her up even more.

'Bye then,' she said, putting the phone down firmly. Honestly, didn't she have enough things on her mind without having to act as lover-boy's messenger?

The old sewing machine that used to belong to her grandmother weighed a ton. Jas's arms ached from dragging it up the stairs to her room. She shoved a pile of magazines off her desk and put the machine in their place.

Then she got out the fabric she'd bought in Peabody's. In the natural light from the window, it looked more mud-coloured than ever. Jas tried laying it out on the pale grey carpet, but there wasn't enough space. Piles of magazines and tapes sprawled over the floor. There was a heap of shoes in one corner and a mound of bags and bits in another.

Her mum had been nagging her for ages to tidy up. She'd even threatened to cut Jas's allowance if the mess didn't disappear. But somehow Jas was never in the right mood to put things away – and she didn't feel like doing it now.

She looked round for a space to work. Her room was quite small, but she loved it. It had a really cool grey and white colour scheme which she'd seen in a magazine article about her favourite pop star, Rory Todd. His house was decorated entirely in shades of white and grey – and if it was good enough for Rory Todd, it was good enough for Jasmine Scott!

Of course, Rory Todd's house was incredibly clean and tidy. But then, Jas reasoned, he probably had a cleaning lady to do all the work for him. Not like her!

She smoothed out the duvet on her bed and laid the mud-coloured fabric on top of it. It wasn't as flat as the floor, but it would do. She tried to remember how they'd cut out garments in the Fashion and Textiles class at school. If she folded the material in two and then drew the shape she wanted and cut it out, she'd get a back and a front piece, which was what she needed.

Jas fetched the black top, on which she'd based her design, from the wardrobe. She laid it out on the fabric. It didn't quite fit. 'Bum!' she exclaimed. Not enough fabric. Never mind, though. She was sure she could work something out. She took a pencil and drew round the black top, as far as she could, then chucked it on the floor and adapted the pencilled shape to fit the space. It looked fine. Once it was sewn together, it would probably be an improvement on the shape of the black top.

Next, it was cutting out time. The scissors were nice and sharp and cut through the layers of fabric easily. Halfway through the job, Jas heard the front door open. Abby must be home. She mustn't forget to give her Stuart's message, but she'd finish the cutting out first.

Jas snipped the last bit of fabric away and picked up the two pieces of her new design. So far, so good, she thought, pleased with herself. All she had to do was sew the back to the front, and she'd got her basic top. What was it Becky had said about the whole idea being too complicated? What did Becky know?

Jas picked up the fabric – and stared in horror as a piece of grey and white material fell to the floor. When she was cutting out the top, she'd snipped a hole in the duvet cover! On closer inspection, there were also two long scissor slashes that gaped open, revealing the duvet inside.

Jas froze. What was she going to do? Her mum would go spare! The duvet cover was only a few weeks old and Mrs Scott had moaned about its cost when she'd bought it.

There was only one thing to do, and that was try and sew it back together again. The slashes wouldn't be too difficult, but the patch she'd snipped out would be more complicated. If she was really careful, it might not show too much. But there wasn't time to do that right away. Getting the top stitched up was the most important thing at the moment.

Jas quickly flipped the duvet over. The pattern was on both sides, so unless someone actually got into the bed, they'd never know what had happened. She put the piece of grey-patterned material into the little cupboard by her bed.

From now on, she'd be more careful. She couldn't afford to make any more mistakes.

3

'Stuart stood me up!'

Even though she was in her own room, Jas heard Abby's wail quite clearly.

Oh no! Jas grimaced as she looked at her watch and saw the time. In her panic about the duvet cover she'd forgotten all about Stuart's message! Abby must have been waiting at the cafe for ages.

Jas opened her bedroom door a crack. From downstairs she could hear the comforting murmur of her mother's voice, and Abby sobbing. 'I can't believe he'd do this to me,' she kept saying.

Jas shut the bedroom door and flung herself on her bed. What was she going to do now? She felt terrible. Her heart told her she should go down now and confess. But that would mean big trouble. Abby would never believe it was a genuine mistake. She'd go mad.

Jas glanced at the mud-coloured fabric hanging from the sewing machine. Nothing had worked out as well as she'd planned and the top looked more like a rag than a prize-winning design. The sewing machine wasn't working properly and the seams had gone all puckered. The shoulders were lopsided, too. Worse than that, the shape was wrong.

Instead of the loose, swingy style she'd been aiming for, the top just hung limply.

If there was one thing she desperately needed it was her big sister's advice, Jas thought. And if she was going to get any of that, she'd better move quickly. She pulled the fabric out of the sewing machine and went downstairs clutching it.

Abby was perched on one of the kitchen worktops with her legs dangling. Her eyes looked puffy and she kept dabbing at them with a wodge of paper towel. Jas felt guilty at seeing her hurt.

'I'm sure there's a perfectly ordinary explanation,' Mrs Scott was saying quietly as she unpacked a pie from its cardboard box and put it in the oven. 'Stuart's not the sort of person who'd let you down like that. I expect he got held up.'

'He's never done it before,' sniffed Abby. 'Don't make any supper for me, Mum. I couldn't eat a thing.'

Mrs Scott turned to Jas, who was standing in the doorway. 'How about you, Jas? Have you had anything yet or do you want some chicken and ham pie?'

Jas's stomach rumbled. She'd been so busy she hadn't even thought about supper. 'Yes, please,' she said, putting her outfit down.

Years ago, before her mum started working, the whole family used to eat together in the evening. But these days, with her parents often getting delayed, it was left to Jas and Abby to help themselves to something when they felt like it.

'Help me top and tail these beans, will you?' asked Mrs Scott, taking a pack from the fridge.

'I'm just going to change out of this suit. My feet are killing me – I haven't stopped racing round all day.'

Jas began snapping the ends off the beans. 'I know you don't want to get involved in this fashion competition I'm going in for,' she said to Abby as she worked, 'but I really need some advice.'

'What's happened?' Abby sighed.

'Look at my outfit.' Jas held it up.

Abby burst into laughter. 'This is supposed to be a prize-winning outfit?' She reached out and took it. 'What is it? A potato sack?'

Jas winced, but she had to admit that it did look pretty awful.

'It's supposed to be a loose, swingy top like my black one,' she explained. 'I didn't have enough material, though, so I had to cheat a bit. And I got the shoulders wrong.'

'You sure did.' Abby was trying to be serious; Jas could tell from the way she'd bitten her lip to stop herself laughing.

'Can I rescue it, do you reckon?'

'Well . . .' Abby pulled a face. 'Maybe. But you should really have cut it out on the bias. That's what gives it a swingy feel.'

'Oh.' Jas wasn't even sure what the bias was.

'And it was a mistake to try and skimp on the fabric.'

'Yeah, I was beginning to think that, too.' Disappointed, Jas turned back to the sink and the beans. 'I'd better just give up.' She felt as if all her plans had suddenly blown up in her face. And wouldn't Liz and Becky and Charlie be amused when she had

36

to admit that her design had been too complicated for her to make – just as they'd predicted.

'You might be able to turn it into a different sort of top. You'd have to unpick your sewing and start again, but I don't think you need to junk it.' Abby held it against herself. 'You could try making it more fitted.'

'Could I?' Jas gazed at the top. It was all very well Abby suggesting what to do, but *how*? 'Do you think you could . . . ?' she started, trying not to sound too hopeful.

'Could what?' Abby's eyes twinkled as she stared at her. 'You want me to do it for you? That sounds a bit like cheating.'

'Not do it for me,' Jas inserted quickly, 'just show me what do do. Otherwise I'll probably just make it even worse.'

Abby held her chin in the air. 'After that trick you pulled on Stuart yesterday, I shouldn't even be speaking to you,' she said. Then she added miserably, 'but now he's stood me up, I've got nothing better do do.'

'It was mean of me to do that with the chilli.' Jas hung her head. Her ears felt hot. It wasn't guilt about yesterday that bothered her as much as forgetting today's message.

Abby sighed. 'Okay, I suppose I might as well give you a hand. Finish those beans and then we'll see what we can do.'

Jas's heart skipped a beat. Today had been a total disaster – but maybe there was a chance of turning it into a success after all. She finished the beans quickly and put them in the colander.

Abby jumped down from the worktop. 'Let's go upstairs and get this started.'

They were halfway up when the doorbell rang. Jas jumped about six inches. She had a pretty good idea who it was.

The game was up. There was no way she could get out of it now. 'Actually, Abby,' she began quickly, 'there's something I forgot to tell you. I got so carried away making that top—'

But Abby wasn't listening. Her whole face had lit up. 'Perhaps that's Stuart,' she said hopefully, racing back down the stairs with her wavy dark hair bouncing round her shoulders. 'Maybe he got held up or something.'

'Yes, he did,' Jas tried to explain, following her sister. 'He called, you see . . .'

Abby flung open the front door. Stuart was standing there. The instant he saw Abby, his face lit up. Then he looked worried. 'Are you all right? I was waiting for you at the cinema – I thought you'd stood me up.'

'I thought *you'd* stood *me* up!' Abby giggled, planting a big kiss on his cheek.

Jas tried to look surprised, but her face felt strained. 'Look, this is my fault,' she muttered.

'You *did* give Abby my message?' Stuart asked, running his fingers through his hair.

Jas tried to keep breathing steadily. 'I'm sorry – I forgot,' she said. 'I was so busy making my top, and with the sewing machine going I didn't hear Abby come in.'

'You mean Stuart called? You *knew* he'd changed our arrangement to meet?' Abby stood there with a stunned look on her face. 'Why didn't you say something when you came downstairs?'

Jas looked down at the mud-coloured rag she was holding. She felt really bad. 'Because I was desperate for some help with this,' she said, holding it out.

Stuart was looking confused, but Abby's eyebrows shot up. 'You mean you let me believe that Stuart had stood me up, just so I'd help you with your outfit?'

There were tears pricking Jas's eyes. 'I'm sorry,' she said, nodding. 'I know I should have told you straight away.'

Abby put her hands on her hips. 'I can't believe what I'm hearing!' she exclaimed angrily. 'Okay, maybe you forgot to give me Stuart's message in the first place, but letting me go on thinking he'd stood me up was a really nasty thing to do.'

'I can see that now,' Jas flushed.

'Only because you got found out,' Abby retorted. 'I've just about had enough of you,' she snapped. 'Yesterday it was that little "accident" you had with Stuart's burger – and today you just forgot to pass on an important message . . . I'm sick of you and your selfish behaviour, Jas. It's like sharing the house with a naughty little kid.'

Jas winced. 'I'm sorry. I was going to tell you.'

'*After* you'd got me to help with your stupid potato sack, I suppose!' Abby drew herself up to her full height. 'I don't understand why you're so jealous of Stuart.'

'Jealous of *him*?' Jas could hardly believe it. Why should she be jealous of Stuart?

'Yes,' Abby nodded firmly. 'It's time you learned

a few lessons, Jas. And number one is, you can forget about asking me any favours. From now on, you're on your own. You can make your own mistakes and you can put them right yourself.'

She took Stuart by the arm. 'Let's go for a walk,' she suggested.

'Sure.' Stuart, still looking stunned, opened the front door and led her out.

Jas watched them walking hand in hand down the road, Abby's head on Stuart's shoulder. As they disappeared round the corner, Jas felt all her hopes disappear too.

Jas was still feeling down the next day when Charlie and Liz came up to her and said hello.

'Hi,' she said, and their smiles confirmed that everything was back to normal.

'Look what I've got,' announced Charlie, flicking her long red hair over her shoulder. She pulled a sheet of paper from her Earth Friends bag.

'Me too,' added Liz, opening her case and extracting one of several neatly labelled folders. *Threads Fashion Contest*, it read on the front. 'See, we do have ideas – we're just a bit slower than you.'

They held out their designs. Charlie's was for a screen-printed T-shirt. 'I picked up on your idea of shells and starfish and added some mermaids,' she said. 'If all our outfits have got a similar idea, they'll look better in the fashion show.'

Jas couldn't argue. It was a good idea. She just wished that Charlie could have been a bit more ambitious with her design.

'What do you think?' Liz asked, pointing to her

picture. It showed some shorts, almost knee length, and a suntop. 'I thought I could paint a few shells and starfish on too – if that's okay with you.'

Before Jas could say anything, Becky came bounding up. Her blonde hair was gathered into a twist on top of her head. 'Take a look at this,' she said, pulling out a thick notepad with a purple and pink striped cover. 'You said we could design something really simple, Jas, so I have.'

'What is it? A bath towel?' Charlie raised her eyebrows.

'It's a sarong,' Becky said defensively. 'It's a big oblong of cotton fabric you wrap round yourself and tie. People wear them on beaches. It couldn't be easier.'

'And no complicated sewing,' nodded Liz.

Jas smiled, despite the fact that her heart had fallen even further into her boots than before. 'They're very nice designs,' she said, sitting down on the grass. The others sat down with her.

'And they're practical and easy to make,' Liz agreed.

'Yes . . .' Jas hesitated. She had a choice. She could either lie and tell them they were wonderful, or she could hold on to her ambition of winning the competition. Which was it going to be?

'Perhaps we could do a few things that will make them more special,' she suggested. She unzipped a pocket in her backpack and got out her pencil case. 'I mean, Liz, if you were to make the shorts of your outfit much shorter, and crop the suntop so you get a bare midriff . . .' She drew a picture of how it might look.

'But I'd have to model these!' Liz looked aghast. 'I couldn't appear in front of the whole school dressed like that. I'd die of embarrassment.'

'Why?' Jas was perplexed. 'You've got great legs.'

Liz went pink. 'It's just not me,' she protested.

'I wouldn't mind,' volunteered Becky. 'Why don't I wear your outfit, Liz, and you can wear my sarong?' But Liz still didn't look pleased.

Jas turned her attention to Charlie's sketch. 'This mermaid design's really great,' she offered. 'It's just – well, it's a bit ordinary. We need to do something special so the judges will be really impressed.' Charlie's eyebrows came down in a straight line of disapproval.

'Go on,' she said, her tone making it clear that Jas was on trial.

'You could do the design all over the T-shirt, maybe,' Jas suggested. 'Or how about silk-screening a more interesting piece of clothing? I mean T-shirts are a bit ordinary, aren't they?'

'I like T-shirts,' retorted Charlie, with a stung look.

'Jas, we're supposed to be working on this as a team,' Liz protested. 'They're supposed to be *our* ideas, not just yours.'

'Yes,' echoed Becky, taking back her drawing of the sarong. Her blue eyes were glittering with irritation. 'I don't want to hear what you've got to say about my idea, Jas.'

Jas held out her hands in exasperation. 'I'm not trying to be horrible,' she insisted. 'I'm just suggesting a few changes that'll make your outfits more exciting.'

Charlie shook her head. 'It feels to me as if you're just trying to boss us around because you think you know more about fashion than we do.'

Jas chewed her gum furiously. 'It's not like that. I just want to see our team win.'

'And you want to be team boss,' Becky said huffily. She put her notepad away. 'Daniel's over by the science block. I think I'll join him.' She got up and walked away.

'Now look what you've done!' Liz said accusingly. 'You've scared Becky off. Why can't you be more tactful, Jas?'

Jas just rolled her eyes. All she wanted to do was improve their chances of winning the contest. But why bother?

'Vale tells me you're planning something ambitious for the fashion contest,' drawled Gina Galloway, perching on the corner of Jas's table in the library.

'That's right,' Jas said, with more confidence than she felt. After all, at the moment her brilliant outfit was nothing more than a bundle of mud-coloured rags.

Gina leaned forward conspiratorially. Her blonde hair floated around her pale face. She was wearing perfume, too. Jas could smell it, flowery and a bit sickly.

'You know that you haven't got a chance if you stick with that bunch of losers.' She nodded to the table where Becky, Liz and Charlie were sitting talking together.

'That's your opinion,' stated Jas.

Gina's silvery eyes gleamed. 'There's room for

one more person on my team, you know. It could be yours if you want it.'

'No way!' Jas picked up the book she'd been pretending to read, and pretended to read it some more. It was difficult to believe she'd heard Gina properly. They'd never been friends. Not exactly enemies, maybe, but Jas just kept out of Gina's way when she could. Why on earth did Gina think she might want to join her team?

'Have you heard of Kiff Rowan?' Gina asked, changing tack suddenly. She was staring at Jas's black jacket. It was the one that had got soaked in the downpour the other day, and it was looking decidedly the worse for wear.

Jas sighed wearily. 'Of course I've heard of Kiff Rowan. He's the best designer around.' Why wouldn't Gina just leave her alone? 'Any more stupid questions?'

'I've got a really gorgeous Kiff Rowan jacket.' Gina peered at her nails, which had a silver-coloured coat of varnish. 'The only problem is, it's black – and I've come to the conclusion that black isn't really my colour.'

Jas silently agreed. In black, Gina would look like a ghost. But black was definitely *Jas's* colour.

Gina seemed to read her mind. 'The jacket doesn't suit me, but it might suit you. And you look as if you could do with a new jacket,' she finished nastily.

'You're so kind,' Jas said sarcastically. Just like Gina to hand out an enticing offer and an insult at the same time. 'But this jacket's fine.'

It wasn't true. Her own jacket had seen better days. It would have to be junked before too long. And she'd love to get her hands on a real Kiff Rowan jacket. She'd seen his clothes in all the fashion magazines, and they were beautiful – and very expensive.

'If you feel like that . . .' Gina shrugged. 'I was just going to suggest you come round and have a look at it – that's all.'

Despite the fact she disliked Gina, Jas felt a dig of disappointment in her stomach. It was a tempting offer. She'd really like to see that jacket. It would be a treat just to try it on. But Gina was the most scheming and untrustworthy person around. She might be lying about the whole thing. Even so, a Kiff Rowan jacket was a Kiff Rowan jacket. And Jas knew she'd never be able to afford one herself in a million years.

'This jacket sounds like a bribe,' she murmured, her mind reeling with thoughts.

'Would I do that?' Gina gave her a coy glance. 'Why don't you come round to my place after school and have a look at it?'

'Well . . .' Jas felt torn. She didn't want to get involved with Gina and her gang, but she felt well and truly hooked. How could she turn a chance like this down? She was unlikely to get a chance to lay her hands on a Kiff Rowan jacket anywhere else. It was too tempting.

'I'll meet you at the end of the school drive,' she breathed, suspecting as she said it that she'd made a terrible mistake.

'See you later, then,' Gina said with a triumphant smile.

'Look,' said Liz, walking across the library as the bell went, 'the three of us have been thinking—'

45

'And you were right to try and jazz up our designs,' finished Charlie.

'Though you could have been a bit lighter with the criticism,' added Becky.

'So we thought it might be a good idea if all four of us got together after school and finished our designs.' Liz adjusted her velvet hairband. 'Why don't we go to Becky's?'

'We're all free,' Becky said with a grin. She nibbled at her fingernail.

Jas nearly choked with surprise at this unexpected change of plans. 'Actually, I'm not,' she said huskily.

'What are you doing?' Liz wanted to know.

'Nothing special, I just can't come out after school.' Jas could feel her ears burning again. The last few days, they'd hardly stopped.

'Well, that's great!' Charlie's voice was half-angry, half-amused. 'We go to the trouble of getting ourselves organised and now *you* can't make it.'

'Can we come round to your place?' Becky suggested. 'It doesn't matter where we meet.'

'No.' Jas shook her head. No way was she going to tell them about Gina. They'd go mad if they suspected.

'Is everything all right?' Liz asked. 'You're looking really mysterious. Remember, we agreed there'd be no secrets between us.'

'It's just that I'm not in Abby's good books at the moment,' Jas muttered. 'I forgot to pass on a message from Stuart, so I'm in the doghouse.'

'Grounded again!' giggled Becky. 'How many times is that in the last few weeks?'

'I'm not really grounded. I can come round and

see you later. I just can't come straight from school,' Jas said.

Liz, Becky and Charlie shrugged. 'Okay, come round when you can. We'll have some new and exciting designs waiting for you when you get there.'

'Great.' Jas smiled – but somehow her pleasure was spoiled by the knowledge that she hadn't told them everything. But she'd manage to work things out – wouldn't she?

4

Gina's house was huge and old – according to Gina, over a hundred years old. The hall was the size of the sitting room in Jas's house. A sparkly chandelier hung down from the high ceiling and in the centre stood a round table with a huge bowl of roses.

Jas stared around at the elegant wallpaper and furniture. It was like going back in time, and a bit overwhelming.

Gina dumped her bag on the black and white tiled floor. 'Mrs Harper!' she called. There was no sound. 'She must have gone out shopping,' Gina concluded. 'We're safe.'

'Good,' said Vale, taking something out of her bag before dumping it beside Gina's.

'Who's Mrs Harper?' Jas asked, following the other two through double doors into a huge sitting room. There were French windows leading on to a terrace and three large sofas covered in chintzy fabric. The walls were hung with paintings.

'She's our housekeeper.' Gina threw herself down on one of the sofas and Vale on another. Jas sat on the edge of the third. Gina's house was like a hotel she'd once stayed in, when the Scotts had gone to a cousin's wedding in Devon.

Vale leaned over and tapped her. 'Cigarette?' She held out an open pack.

'No, thanks.' Jas noticed that Vale was already holding one herself.

'I will,' laughed Gina, taking one. 'It really helps you relax after a hard day at school.'

She reached out for a silver box on a table by the sofa. It was full of matches. She lit one and started puffing on the cigarette. Vale, too, had lit up.

'Why don't you smoke?' Vale looked surprised. 'I mean you look pretty cool.' Her eyes strayed over Jas's black mini-skirt and stretchy black top.

'My parents are very anti-smoking. My grandad died of lung cancer, you see,' Jas explained, feeling uncomfortable. 'It's the one thing my parents are really strict about.'

Gina shrugged. 'I guess old people have to die of something.'

Jas was shocked. What a terrible thing to say. 'Where do you get your cigarettes from?' she asked. 'I thought it was illegal for people to sell them to kids under sixteen.'

Vale laughed. 'I don't have to buy them. My parents smoke and they buy a few hundred from the supermarket every week. Or my dad brings them back duty-free when he goes abroad with his job. They never notice if a few packets go missing.' She and Gina giggled conspiratorially.

'Want a drink?' Gina got up from the sofa and went over to a big antique cabinet. She opened the door to reveal rows of bottles and glasses.

Jas could hardly believe it. There was a bottle of sherry and some whisky in one of the kitchen cupboards at home, for when visitors came, but nothing like this. This was like a bar. She had no idea what was in most of the bottles.

'Gin and tonic, vodka, beer? Or how about a cocktail?' Gina stood there with a smirking smile on her pale face.

Jas gulped. She didn't drink alcohol – but she didn't want to seem uncool in front of these two. 'What are you going to have?' she asked.

Gina's smirk grew. 'You're my guest, you choose first.' Jas looked along the rows of coloured and clear bottles. Nothing looked very nice.

'I'll just have a Coke, please,' she muttered, feeling stupid.

'Okay.' Gina shut the cabinet. 'Coke's in the fridge. 'We'll have some too.' She shot a knowing smile at Vale and the two of them giggled.

They were teasing her, Jas realised as she followed them down a long corridor to the kitchen. It was horrible, feeling that they were playing games. Jas felt intimidated.

The kitchen was just as big as the other rooms and decorated to look like an old farmhouse. There were wooden units everywhere and a huge red stove. Baskets of vegetables sat out on display, alongside arrangements of dried flowers. 'It's amazing!' Jas said as she stared round.

Gina smiled and took a long puff on her cigarette. 'I know. It's been featured in *Beautiful Homes* magazine. My mother said that when the photographer arrived to take the pictures, he said it was the most perfect kitchen he'd seen. I think he was right, don't you?'

Jas nodded, wishing she'd never said anything. Gina Galloway had a high enough opinion of herself anyway; she didn't need anyone to bolster it.

Gina went over to the fridge, which was carefully hidden behind a wooden door, and took out three Cokes. 'Let's go up to my room,' she suggested.

Jas followed obediently. There was a long landing with lots of doors leading off each side. Gina opened one. 'Come and have a look at this Kiff Rowan jacket I was telling you about.'

Gina's bedroom was just as big and glamorous as the rest of the house. She had an old-fashioned brass bedstead and lots of cuddly toys and frilly cushions everywhere. In one corner there was a TV. Vale went and turned it on, then settled on some cushions and lit another cigarette.

'Through here, Jas,' Gina called. She'd disappeared through a door into another small room lined with wardrobes. Through another door on the far side, Jas could see a bathroom.

'Do you have your own dressing-room?' Gina asked, opening a wardrobe to display racks of clothes.

'Not really,' muttered Jas, thinking of her own room.

'Never mind,' said Gina, flicking through some of the outfits. 'These are my jackets. The Kiff Rowan one has to be here somewhere.'

Jas tried not to look too impressed, but it was difficult. Gina had dozens of jackets – and dozens of everything else, too. One or two of them Jas recognised, but not many.

'When do you get time to wear all these things?' she asked incredulously, watching a leather jacket

51

and a beautiful button-through dress go by, closely followed by a pair of suede jodhpurs and a pink silk blouse.

Gina tucked a strand of fluffy yellow hair behind one ear. 'Weekends, holidays . . . some of them I don't get round to wearing much at all. My mum is always buying me things.'

Jas raised her eyebrows. She wished her mum would do the same!

'Ah, here's the Kiff Rowan jacket.' Gina pulled it out. 'Why don't you try it on?'

It didn't take much encouragement. Jas slipped off her own black jacket and slid her arms into the one Gina held out. It was difficult to believe that two black jackets could be so different. The Kiff Rowan one felt as soft as a cloud. It was tailored at the waist and hips and had lovely buttons. At the points of the collar and on the cuffs there was a very discreet embroidered logo.

Jas looked at herself in the mirror. She'd been instantly transformed from a schoolgirl into a chic, stylish young woman. She felt totally different.

'It's incredible,' she breathed, stroking the fabric. She'd do anything to own a jacket like this.

'Yeah, it is, isn't it?' Gina nodded. 'It's a few weeks since I tried it on. Let me have a look.'

Reluctantly Jas slid out of the jacket and handed it to Gina. It fitted her just as well as it had Jas, but the colour made Gina look just like a ghost. She twirled in the mirror. 'I don't know, but maybe I could get to like it after all.'

Jas felt her heart hit the ground. She'd thought Gina had said . . . But then she stopped herself.

Gina hadn't promised anything, had she? She'd just implied that Jas could have the jacket. Jas could have kicked herself. She'd fallen for Gina's little games yet again!

'Well, thanks for showing me the jacket.' Jas picked up her own and put it on, hoping she was concealing the bitter disappointment she was feeling.

'Do you have to go so soon?' Gina pouted. Jas was pretty sure she could see a calculating gleam in her silvery eyes.

'Yeah,' she said, grabbing her backpack. Gina followed her back to the bedroom, where Vale was still watching TV. Gina went over and lit another cigarette.

'Before you go, come and have a look in here.' She opened another door on the landing. It was lined with cupboards. At one end was an ironing board, at the other a table with the flashiest, most high-tech sewing machine Jas had ever seen.

'This is the linen room,' Gina explained. Jas felt as if she were on a guided tour of a stately home. 'This is where Mrs Harper does the sewing and repairs.'

Jas nodded, not sure what to say. In one corner was a big basket filled with multi-coloured fabrics. 'What's that?' Jas asked, pointing.

Gina laughed. 'When my mother goes abroad anywhere, she buys lengths of fabrics to be turned into cushions or tablecloths or blouses or anything she fancies. But they usually just pile up in here and nothing's made of them.'

'Can I have a look?'

'Sure.' Gina blew a stream of smoke over her.

Jas sorted through the basket. There were all

kinds of things. She picked up a length of splodgy purple batik print. 'That's from the West Indies,' Gina commented. 'We were there last Christmas.'

Jas put it down again. She didn't want to give Gina any more opportunity to boast. Something shone hazily from the bottom of the basket. She picked it out. It was a length of beautiful golden silk, the colour of a sunny beach. It gleamed magically as she held it out.

'My mum probably bought that in Hong Kong,' Gina said matter-of-factly.

But Jas wasn't listening. She didn't care where it came from. All she knew was that it would be perfect for her fashion show outfit. Starting with something as beautiful as this, she couldn't go wrong.

'Do you like it?' Gina asked.

'It's wonderful,' Jas nodded, folding it up.

'You can have it if you want.' Gina blew a smoke ring. 'My mum said that the people on my team can use anything here.' She stared straight into Jas's eyes. 'How about it? There's one place left.'

'Who else is on the team?' Jas asked, trying to give herself time to think.

'Vale and her friend Isabel from 3C.' Jas knew Isabel. She was a nice rather quiet girl.

She breathed in sharply. She'd suspected that Gina had asked her over to try and entice her on to her team. But she hadn't expected that she'd be seriously tempted. That silk, though . . . And the sewing machine . . .

In the silence as she stood hesitating, footsteps came tapping along the corridor. 'Gina!' a voice called.

'Hell!' Gina frowned and tried to find a place to hide the cigarette. It was too late, though. The linen room door was opening. Before Jas realised what had happened, Gina had shoved the burning cigarette between her fingers. She stared down at it, appalled.

'Hello, darling.' Mrs Galloway, immaculately dressed in peach trousers and a loose jacket, came in. Her cream-coloured hair was held back in an elegant French pleat. 'I thought I might find you here, working on your fashion project.'

She smiled at Jas and raised a questioning eyebrow. 'This is Jas,' Gina drawled. 'She's going to be in my team.'

'Pleased to meet you.' Mrs Galloway sniffed. 'I can smell smoke, Gina.' She looked around. 'Mrs Harper hasn't left the iron on, I hope.'

'No, it's Jas. She was dying for a cigarette,' Gina chipped in smartly.

Jas's eyebrows shot up. 'But I don't . . .' She was silenced by a swift pinch from Gina.

Mrs Galloway frowned. 'I don't approve of smoking upstairs, Jas – and I certainly don't approve of under-age smoking. Please put your cigarette out.'

'But it wasn't—'

'You can stub it out on here,' Gina interrupted, offering her a saucer in which a pot plant had been sitting. Jas did as she was told, though she was inwardly boiling with fury. Gina had set her up to save her own skin. She glared intently at her, but Gina still managed to look the picture of innocence.

Mrs Galloway jangled her car keys. 'I have to go to the airport to pick up daddy now,' she said. 'Do you want to come too, Gina?'

Gina shook her head. 'No, I have homework to do.'

Mrs Galloway beamed at her, totally fooled by her daughter's act. 'Good girl. I'll see you later – and perhaps daddy will have a present for you.'

'I hope so,' Gina said sweetly as her mum shut the door.

'How could you do that to me?' Jas hissed the moment the coast was clear. 'You know I don't smoke!'

But Gina was looking calm. She put her hand on Jas's arm. 'Thanks for getting me out of a scrape. I would have been in big trouble if my mum knew it was me smoking that cigarette.'

'That's your problem,' Jas snapped back. 'Why did you have to pass the blame on to me? Now she thinks *I* smoke.'

'Don't worry about it.' Gina grinned. 'Look, to show you how grateful I am, why don't you borrow that Kiff Rowan jacket for a while?'

Jas's anger froze as she remembered how good the jacket had looked and felt. 'You really mean it?'

'Sure.' Gina led the way back to her room. 'Come and get it.'

Jas hesitated – but only for a second. After all, Gina owed her a favour, didn't she?

'Hey, I thought you were going to come round to my place last night.' Becky flopped down on the grass at Jas's side. 'We waited ages and you didn't show.'

Jas's ears began to get hot. She'd planned to pop round to Becky's after she left Gina's, but somehow it had been difficult to get away from Gina and Vale and their talk of the fashion contest.

'I got held up,' she said apologetically, offering Becky a stick of chewing-gum and taking one for herself. 'Sorry. I did mean to come, but it was getting too late.'

'You missed a great time.' Becky tossed her blonde hair. 'We had a total rethink of all our designs and came up with something completely new. I think even you'll be impressed.' She waved at Liz and Charlie, who were approaching across the playground.

As they came up, Gina Galloway strolled past from the opposite direction. 'Hi, Jas,' she called.

Jas rolled her eyes with embarrassment. 'Hi, Gina.' She tried not to sound too friendly.

Gina stopped and stared. 'Not wearing your new jacket today?'

Jas's ears felt as if they'd explode in flames. 'No,' she said cagily. 'It's too nice for school.'

'I know, it's just gorgeous, isn't it?' Gina grinned – the kind of grin that showed too many teeth to be really friendly.

'Yeah,' agreed Jas, aware that Becky, Charlie and Liz were all earwigging like crazy.

'You must come round to my house again some time. Let's plan something later.' Gina strolled on by, heading for Vale and her other cronies, who were gathered further along the bank.

'What was that about?' asked Becky, with a shrewd glance. 'Have you been round to Gina's house?'

'I just popped round to look at something,' Jas muttered, wishing the ground would open up and swallow her.

'What were you doing at Gina's?' Liz wanted to know. 'Was that where you were last night?'

'And what's this jacket she's talking about?' Becky demanded. 'What's been going on?'

Jas sighed. How had she got into this mess? She should have known she could never get away with it. When her friends got their teeth into something, they didn't let go easily.

'It's nothing. Gina just lent me one of her old jackets, that's all,' she said, trying to change the subject. 'Why don't you show me these new designs you've done?'

But the others weren't going to fall for that.

'You took Gina's jacket?' Charlie was aghast. 'Are you telling me you actually went to Gina Galloway's house and borrowed her old clothes?' Angrily, she picked a dandelion flower and pulled its head off.

'It wasn't like that,' Jas tried to explain.

But the others weren't in the mood for listening to explanations. 'How could you do that?' Liz asked. 'You knew we were waiting for you at Becky's.'

'I got delayed. Mrs Galloway came in and—' Jas shut up. It was best to keep the smoking incident a secret.

Charlie was tying up her long hair with a scarf. 'I bet Gina's trying to get you on her team for the fashion contest,' she said.

'She did ask,' Jas admitted. 'But I wouldn't.'

Liz made a disapproving sound. 'Maybe not yet, but if you've started taking bribes from her . . .'

'It wasn't a bribe,' Jas protested, wishing she could explain to Liz about the cigarette. But Liz wouldn't like *that*, either. She disapproved of smoking.

'Maybe you want to join her team?' Becky's blue eyes were serious. 'Do you, Jas?'

Jas looked hurt. 'You know I don't like Gina. She's sneaky.'

'I can't believe you'd stand us up while you go round to see Gina.' Charlie frowned. 'You said you had to go home yesterday because of Abby.' She bit her lip.

Jas felt terrible – really guilty. 'I knew if I told you about going to Gina's, you wouldn't understand.'

Liz was looking upset. 'There was no need to lie about it,' she said gently. 'There isn't a law against going to visit Gina.'

'Why did you want to go there?' Becky wanted to know. She nibbled her thumbnail anxiously. 'Why choose to see Gina instead of us?'

Jas felt pressured. Her friends seemed to have very little faith in her. And that annoyed her.

'Because she's interested in fashion, for a start,' she blurted out. 'And she likes my ideas.'

'And we don't?' Liz said indignantly.

'No, all you did was criticise when you saw my design.' Jas was getting fed up with all this cross-examining.

'We were just trying to be practical,' Charlie said, her cheeks reddening.

'You were horrible about it!' Jas insisted.

Liz suddenly banged her fist down on the grass. 'I'm getting really sick of this. From the minute this contest was announced, we've done nothing but fight. Maybe it would be best for everyone if you went off and joined Gina's team, Jas.'

'But I don't want that!' Jas protested.

'You just said we're critical and horrible,' Becky retorted, her blue eyes glittering furiously. 'If Gina's so much more appreciative than we are, you'll have a great time with her.'

'But I don't like Gina!' It felt as if the whole situation was escalating beyond Jas's control. Nothing she said seemed to make much difference. It was as if the other three had already made up their minds about her.

'You don't seem to like us much, either,' Liz said pointedly.

'We can always ask Emma to join us,' mused Charlie. 'I know she's looking for a team with a spare place.'

Jas looked helplessly from one furious face to the next. Why should she swallow her pride and beg them to keep her on the team? She hadn't done anything wrong, had she?

'All right,' she said in her husky tone, unable to hide the hurt in her brown eyes. 'If that's the way you feel, I'll join Gina's team.'

And it was all for the best, she figured as she walked away across the playground. Gina was right about Liz and Charlie and Becky being losers. When they appeared at the fashion show in their T-shirts and sarongs, and found themselves up against Gina's team, they'd realise what a mistake they'd made in chucking her out!

5

Mrs Fry, the gym teacher, stood at the entrance to the girls' changing room. 'Come on, you lazy lot!' she shouted as the girls of 2K filed in. 'It's a lovely day out there. I think we'll start with a circuit of the sports field to warm everyone up.'

Jas heard Charlie's loud groan. Charlie hated gym class, and especially running. Jas, on the other hand, enjoyed it. She was a fast runner, when she was in the mood. Right now, though, she had something else on her mind.

Where was Gina? She had to find her and tell her she'd decided to join her team. She looked round the changing room. A tuft of blonde fluff waggling above the top of one of the lockers caught her eye.

'Gina, I need to talk to you!' Jas bounded round the lockers.

'Oh, hi.' Gina stopped chatting to Lucy Groves and glanced up. Far from being enthusiastic, her eyes seemed to look straight through Jas. There was none of the friendliness she'd shown earlier.

'Can I have a word with you?' Jas felt rattled. She'd expected Gina to be pleased to see her.

Gina shrugged. Her silvery eyes had an icy glint. 'I suppose so. I'm talking to Lucy right now, though. I'll speak to you later, okay?'

Jas nodded, feeling numb, and went back across the changing room to find a space along the benches. Usually she sat with her friends, but this morning that was out of the question. She untied her shoes and pulled on her black leggings.

All the while, her mind ran round and round, trying to work out what was going on. Why was Gina suddenly acting so cold? She couldn't have changed her mind, could she? Jas's blood froze. After the row they'd had, it was impossible to go back to the gang. But if Gina wouldn't have her, she'd be left without a team. And the rules of the competition were that everyone competed in a team of four. Unless she could get into a team, Jas might as well give up her hopes of winning here and now.

In a moment of panic she looked round the changing room. Everyone had already divided up into teams – everyone who was going to take part, anyway. Ryan Bryson's team still had two spaces left but Jas could never work with Ryan and his friend Sean. They only wanted to go in for the contest to show off and be silly.

If she couldn't join Gina's team, she'd be out of the competition altogether . . .

'Having second thoughts?'

Jas whirled round and almost swept her plate from her lunch tray. 'Oh, Becky,' she said, trying to hide her disappointment. She'd hoped it was someone else. 'You haven't seen Gina anywhere, have you?'

Becky smiled knowingly. 'No, but I've seen you looking everywhere for her. What's happened?'

Jas ignored the question and helped herself to a

yoghurt from the lunch counter. She was feeling pretty desperate. Desperate enough to forget her pride.

'About this morning's disagreement,' she began. 'I don't suppose we could . . . ?'

'It's too late to change anything now.' Becky got out her purse to pay the cashier. 'Emma's decided to join us, so our team's full.' She nodded across the crowded dining-hall to a huddle of heads bent over something.

Jas instantly recognised Charlie's cascade of auburn hair and Liz's gleaming honey-coloured bob. 'We're just finalising our designs. We start work on them after school.' Becky informed Jas. 'And Emma seems to fit right in with us, so we shouldn't have any problems.'

'Right.' Jas nodded and watched as Becky manoeuvred her way between the chairs and joined the others. She suddenly felt like the loneliest person in the world.

Things couldn't possibly get any worse, Jas thought as she scuttled through the main reception area of the school, with its wooden panelling and plaster friezes round the top of the walls. But they could, as she discovered when the staff room door opened and Miss Tyler came out, beaming.

'Jasmine!' she called, ushering another person out of the room. 'I've had a visitor – someone you know.' Jas stopped and tucked her chewing-gum safely into her cheek.

'Hello, Stuart,' she said grimly, noting that at least he was wearing some decent black jeans today, and not the dreaded pink bermuda shorts that made his legs look like hairy matchsticks. Fortunately, too, there was no one else around to see him.

Stuart smiled radiantly. 'Hi, Jas. I wanted to thank you for telling me about the fashion show. I've just arranged with Miss Tyler to be the official photographer.'

'It was an excellent idea of yours to suggest that Stuart take photos of the show,' added Miss Tyler.

Jas raised her eyebrows. It hadn't been her idea at all! She'd actively tried to put him off. She glared at him and he gave her a barely perceptible wink.

'Having a professional photographer will make the fashion show a really special occasion,' Miss Tyler went on. She was positively glowing – just like Abby when she was with Stuart. What was it about him that made strong women go all flushed and gooey? Jas wondered.

'He's not a professional yet,' she pointed out, knowing it must sound cheeky.

'I'm sure he's much more professional than me with my Instamatic.' Miss Tyler laughed, and her red and gold earrings swung backwards and forwards.

'We'll need to have some lights set up.' Stuart was suddenly serious. 'Can we black out the hall? It would be much more dramatic that way.'

'No problem,' said Miss Tyler.

'I'll come in on the Friday morning with my lights and get everything set up, then,' Stuart said. 'Abby's volunteered to be my assistant, and I might bring another photography student from college, if that's okay?'

Jas felt more annoyed than ever. Abby and Stuart

together was bad enough. But the pair of them together at school – on *her* territory – was even worse.

Stuart grinned at her. 'And I promise to take some really stunning pictures of your outfit,' he said enthusiastically.

'Jas is very creative,' Miss Tyler said, nodding. 'And she dresses so stylishly.'

Jas did a double-take. She'd lost count of the times Miss Tyler had commented on how short her skirts were, or reminded her that the school uniform colour was blue, not her favourite black. What had come over her?

'I know Jas is taking the competition really seriously,' Stuart told Miss Tyler. 'I wouldn't be surprised if she walks off with first prize.'

They were being so nice – but all Jas wanted to do was disappear off the face of the earth. After all, the way things were going, she wouldn't be appearing in Stuart's photos at all!

As she walked down the drive on her way home that afternoon, Jas caught sight of a familiar fuzz of cream hair bobbing along a hundred yards ahead. 'Gina!' she called, and sprinted down the drive, fixing a confident smile on her face as she ran.

'I've been looking for you all day!' Jas began cheerfully, as if they'd already agreed that she join Gina's team. 'When do we get down to work on our outfits?'

Gina tipped her head to one side. 'I don't know what you're talking about,' she said innocently. 'You're not in my team.'

Jas tried to keep the smile on her face, even though it felt unnatural. 'Well, you asked me yesterday and I thought it over – and I've decided it would be a good idea. You were right about Becky and the others being losers. I want to win the competition. So when do we start?'

Gina raised one shoulder in a helpless gesture. 'I just don't understand,' she said in a wheedling little voice, like the one she'd used with her mother the previous day. 'I didn't think you liked me. You hardly managed to speak to me this morning – even though I let you borrow my jacket.' She managed a wounded look.

Jas's smile faded. She was being manipulated, and she knew it. Under that fluffy, pale exterior Gina was as hard as nails. She was only playing at being hurt. But if Jas wanted to get on to Gina's team she knew she'd have to play along – and grovel.

The thought of it made her shudder. For two years she'd shared a classroom with Gina and watched her swanking around, boasting and showing off. She remembered the way Gina had picked on Emma Pennington when they went on the adventure trip to Wales. She remembered all the times Gina had bad-mouthed people and put them down.

Could she really crawl to her? Jas didn't want to – but what option did she have? She opened her mouth and tried to say sorry, but nothing came out except a throaty growl. She coughed and tried again. 'I'm sorry.' It didn't sound right.

'I don't know.' Gina pouted. 'I just don't think we'd get on if we were in the same team.'

'I think we would,' Jas muttered. Then she threw

66

away all her pride. 'I think you'd make a great team leader, Gina.'

'Do you really?' Gina drew herself up proudly. 'I guess I would!'

Jas nodded. Her humiliation was complete. 'Well, if you realise that . . . Do you really want to be in my team?' Gina asked.

'Yes,' Jas managed. It was Gina's team or nothing – and Gina was better than nothing, though only just.

'Badly?' Gina was smirking now.

'Yeah. It's the best team. You're going to win the competition, no question.' Jas forced the words out.

'And you'll help with ideas for the rest of us, and give us a hand with the sewing?' Gina asked.

'Sure, I'll do anything.' Jas looked down at Gina's brand-new shoes. Right now, she was so desperate she'd even kiss her feet if that was what Gina requested.

'Okay!' Gina sighed. 'You can join.'

Jas breathed a sigh of relief, even though she suspected that her troubles were only just beginning. 'That's great.'

'I'm meeting Vale and Isabel at my house,' Gina announced, 'so you'd better come along.'

Jas fell into step by her side. At least she was a member of a team again. For that, at least, she should be grateful.

'Why don't you try one?' Vale held out the packet of cigarettes. The four of them were lounging around in Gina's bedroom, with the compact disc player blaring loudly.

'No, thanks.' Jas shook her head.

Gina leaned over and took a cigarette and so, to Jas's surprise, did Isabel. She wouldn't have suspected that Isabel was the kind of girl who smoked. She was quiet and less brash than the other two.

'There's no need to worry about getting caught,' said Gina, borrowing Vale's plastic lighter and taking her first puff. 'My mum's in London and won't be back till eight, and Mrs Harper's gone home early.'

'It's not that,' Jas replied – though she certainly didn't want to get caught by Mrs Galloway a second time. 'I just don't like smoking.'

Vale laughed. 'Well, you'll have to get used to it if you want to be in our team. We're not giving up just for you.'

Isabel, sitting beside Gina, took a long drag on her cigarette and then burst into a fit of coughing. 'I haven't been smoking long,' she gasped, 'but it's relaxing.'

Jas frowned. It didn't seem that relaxing to be sitting there coughing your lungs up.

'Of course, you're only a second year,' Vale said scathingly. 'You're too immature to appreciate grown-up things like smoking.'

'I'm not immature!' protested Jas. 'Smoking's a bad habit. I bet in a few years' time you'll wish you'd never started.'

Vale exploded with giggles. 'You sound just like my mum!' she laughed. 'She's always telling me not to smoke. She keeps saying that if she'd known what a horrible habit it was when she was young, she'd never have had a cigarette.'

'Well, it is a bad habit,' said Jas. 'It's disgusting and a total waste of money. You might as well just light a five-pound note and watch it go up in smoke.'

'Doesn't cost us anything!' Vale laughed some more. Her face was even redder than usual.

Gina leaned over, a cunning expression on her face. 'How do you know it's so terrible if you've never tried it? Or do you just believe everything your parents tell you?'

'No!' Jas cried, stung. 'Anyway, that's stupid. It's like saying that until you've been run over by a car, you can't be sure it hurts.'

Gina wasn't giving up, though. 'I bet you do everything your mum and dad tell you,' she said, leaning back among the pillows on her bed.

Vale gave another low laugh. The pair of them were making Jas really self-conscious. 'They don't like me chewing gum, but I still do it,' she responded.

'Maybe, but chewing gum isn't illegal, is it?' Gina looked triumphantly at the other two. 'She's chicken, that's all! She's hiding behind her mum and dad because she's too scared to try smoking.'

'I'm not scared,' Jas growled resentfully. 'I just don't like smoking, okay?'

'Chicken,' laughed Gina. 'You're scared.'

Jas folded her arms. 'I didn't come here to argue about cigarettes,' she said firmly. 'Why don't we get working on our outfits? I haven't seen your ideas yet.'

But Gina wasn't going to let her off the hook. 'Take one little puff to prove you're not chicken,' she urged, holding out her cigarette. 'One puff – it won't hurt you.'

'No,' Jas insisted.

Gina looked disappointed. 'Are you sure you really want to be in my team, Jas?'

Jas flinched. This was blackmail. 'I wouldn't be here if I didn't want to be in the team, would I?'

Vale joined in. 'Maybe you're not the right person for the team. Perhaps we should look for someone who isn't so pig-headed about smoking.'

'I'm not pig-headed about it!' Jas knew she was in a no-win situation. They were determined to turn everything she said against her.

'Prove it.' Gina took a fresh cigarette from the packet and lit it, then held it out to Jas. 'One cigarette. That's all you have to smoke.'

Jas frowned. 'But just now you said I only had to take one puff.'

'I changed my mind,' Gina said with a sneaky smile. 'You'd better smoke this now, before I change my mind again.'

Jas stared at the glowing red ash at the tip of the cigarette. What harm could a few puffs do? She'd never have to smoke another one. And if it shut Gina and Vale up, it would be worth it. She reached out and took it.

'Just give it a gentle suck and then breathe the smoke into your lungs,' Gina instructed.

Jas sucked. The smoke went up her nose and burned her throat. Then she began to choke and her eyes streamed. Vale and Gina laughed as she coughed and spluttered uncontrollably. Isabel slapped her on the back and offered her a tissue.

'It's horrible the first time, isn't it?' she said sympathetically. 'I thought I was going to be sick.'

'I think I *am*,' groaned Jas. Her throat felt scorched and sore.

'Take another drag quickly,' Gina insisted.

'It gets easier,' Isabel reassured her.

Jas, looking doubtful, took another puff. Despite what they said, the smoke still stung. It was horrible. But at least this time she didn't choke.

'See what I mean?' trumpeted Gina. 'You made all that fuss, but I bet you liked it really.'

Jas didn't get a chance to reply, because the doorbell rang. Vale and Gina hurriedly stubbed out their cigarettes on the saucer Gina had brought up from the kitchen. Jas did the same. She didn't want a repeat of the previous day.

'Let's have a look.' Gina opened her bedroom window, which was above the front door, and looked down. She quickly drew her head back in. 'It's Lucy Groves!' she whispered, ducking back inside.

'We could pretend not to be here,' suggested Vale. 'Maybe she'll just go away.'

'What's the problem?' Jas asked. Why should they be acting so strangely about Lucy?

Vale looked at Jas as if she was stupid. 'Gina asked Lucy to join the team for the fashion show.'

'But there isn't a place for her any more.'

Jas looked puzzled – until she remembered seeing Gina and Lucy talking together in the gym changing room.

Gina grimaced. 'I know the best way to handle her.' She leaned out of the window. 'Hi, Lucy!' she called down.

Vale peered out of the other window, giggling. Jas could hear Lucy shouting something back. 'Don't

71

bother,' called Gina, 'I've decided not to have you on my team after all. I've picked Jas instead.'

'That's not fair!' they heard Lucy complain.

'That's life!' yelled Gina, before shutting the window firmly.

'We didn't want her anyway, she's got terrible spots,' commented Vale. 'They would have looked bad in the fashion show. Even so, you were a bit tough on her Gina.'

Isabel was looking concerned. 'Lucy's ever so sweet. I bet that really hurt,' she said quietly.

'She'll survive,' Gina said cheerfully. 'It'll probably do her good – toughen her up.'

Jas felt dreadful. She went to the window in time to see Lucy running down the drive of the house, wiping her hand across her face as if she was crying. For a minute Jas wanted to tell Gina how rotten she was.

But something stopped her. If she was going to win the fashion show, she'd got to toughen up. She couldn't allow herself to go round feeling sorry for everyone who got in Gina's way.

To win, you had to be tough. If you were nice, you ended up a loser. And Jas didn't want to be a loser.

'Great!' Jas sat back on her heels and admired all the sketches they'd produced. Gina's Caribbean-style outfit, with its halter top and split skirt, would look good in the multi-coloured fabric her mother had brought back from Jamaica. Isabel planned to make a white dress and paint a pattern of sandcastles and buckets and spades on it. And Vale had found two pieces of fabric, one with red and white stripes and one with white stars on a blue background, to make an outfit with an 'American vacation' theme.

Jas was delighted. They'd certainly look better than Charlie's printed T-shirt or Liz's baggy shorts. There was just one problem.

'I think we'd better get some paper patterns to help us cut out the shapes,' Jas mused. 'It's not as easy as it looks.' She didn't tell them that the original version of her design had ended up looking like a crumpled sack.

Gina shrugged. 'That's no problem. Mrs Harper will do it. She's brilliant at all those kind of things. She does all the sewing and alterations for us. If you leave the design of your outfit and the fabric you want it in, she'll work out the technical bits and cut it out for you.'

'We'd better leave some measurements for her, then,' added Vale, tapping the ash from her cigarette into the saucer. There were seven cigarette ends in it, Jas noticed.

Gina went across the landing to the linen room and came back with the tape measure. 'Open the windows,' she ordered when she returned. 'It stinks of smoke in here and my mum will be back in half an hour.'

Isabel obediently opened the windows and tried wafting some of the smoke out. Jas, meanwhile, was thinking.

'Are you sure it's okay for Mrs Harper to help us with the outfits?' she asked.

'Why not?' Gina said casually. 'We designed them, didn't we?'

Vale added, 'I bet the other kids are getting some help, too.'

Remembering how she'd asked Abby for help, Jas silenced her worries.

'Tomorrow's Saturday, so why don't we go into town and get all the things we need for the outfits?' Vale suggested. 'You two need fabric paint,' she said nodding to Jas and Isabel, 'and I fancy some big gold earrings and a sun hat.'

'I don't have much money,' Jas confessed, feeling sheepish. Hanging around with Vale and Gina, who didn't seem to think twice about spending money, had made her feel really poor.

Gina looked up from jotting down measurements on her sketch. 'You don't have to worry about cash. I told you that to start with.'

'Why don't we meet at the end of Oakwood Drive at ten o'clock tomorrow?' suggested Isabel. 'Then we can go into town together.'

Jas nodded, impressed. Being in Gina's team made everything so easy!

6

Jas looked in the fridge. There wasn't much there. Her mum usually went to the supermarket early on Saturday morning and bought most of the things they needed for the week. By Friday night, though, supplies were running low. Luckily there was some left-over lasagne in a dish.

'How long shall I put this in the microwave for?' she asked, wandering into the sitting room where Abby was watching TV.

Abby ignored her. She'd been ignoring Jas ever since she'd forgotten Stuart's message. Jas frowned. There was no one else to ask. Her mum and dad had gone to play badminton, as they usually did on Fridays.

She tried again. 'Abby, how long do you think this needs? I don't want to die of food poisoning.'

'Don't let me stop you,' Abby growled. Then she relented. 'Give it four minutes on full, then check and see how it's doing.' She sniffed. 'Where have you been?'

'Over at Gina Galloway's. Why?'

'Because you smell of smoke!' Abby rose from the leather armchair she'd been lounging in and sniffed suspiciously at Jas's black shirt. Jas jumped

75

backwards, but Abby grabbed her and held on. 'Let's smell your breath,' she insisted.

'No!' Jas squeaked, wrenching her head away. She'd planned to chew a piece of gum on her way home, to disguise any smoke on her breath, but – wouldn't you believe it – she'd run out.

Abby kept sniffing. Then she let Jas go. 'You've been smoking!' she accused. 'Jas, how could you be so stupid?'

'I'm not,' Jas replied sulkily. 'And I wasn't smoking, the others were.' She went into the kitchen to get away, but Abby followed her.

'What are you doing hanging around with kids who smoke? I thought your crowd were more mature than that.'

'Stop bugging me,' Jas protested, slamming the microwave door. 'I told you, it's not me who's been smoking.' The few little puffs she'd taken didn't count as smoking, she reasoned to herself.

'I can still smell it on you.' Abby shook her head disbelievingly. 'Don't you know how many people die each year of lung cancer and all the other problems smoking causes?'

'Yes,' Jas replied flatly, fixing her gaze on the lasagne, revolving slowly on its turntable in the oven. 'Mum's told me loads of times.'

'Then why don't you listen?' Abby exploded. 'Smoking's disgusting, Jas! It fills your lungs with tar and ruins your heart. Not only that, it poisons everyone else around you, too. And it turns your teeth and fingers yellow.'

'You want to see my fingers?' Jas shot back, holding out her hands. Why did Abby have to treat her like a little kid? Jas knew all the arguments against smoking. Hadn't she tried to use them on Gina and Vale?

'Just leave it, will you?' she said flatly. She could feel tears gathering under her eyelids. 'I'm getting enough hassle from Gina and her friends. I had a couple of puffs to shut them up, that was all, and I didn't like it.'

Abby's expression changed to concern. 'If they're giving you a hard time, you don't have to hang out with them. What's happened to Liz and Charlie? I bet they don't smoke.'

'I've had a row with them,' Jas admitted grudgingly.

'Well maybe you should make it up with them,' said Abby, pushing back her fringe of glossy dark hair. 'This Gina sounds like a bad influence.'

'Don't start treating me like one of your little kids at the nursery,' Jas groaned.

'Well that's the only way to treat people who smoke,' Abby snapped back. 'There's a girl at college who smokes a pack a day and thinks she looks really cool. She's always moaning that she's got no money, when in fact she's blowing nearly a thousand pounds a year on cigarettes.'

'I'm not going to start smoking.' Jas was tight-lipped. Since Abby had studied health education as part of her college course, she'd got really uptight about things like smoking and eating plenty of green vegetables. Jas hated it. What had happened to the easy-going sister she used to know?

'I don't want to get too heavy on you, Jas,' Abby warned. 'I accept what you say about just having a puff to shut Gina up. But if you come in smelling of smoke again, I'll have to tell Mum and Dad.'

'You can't do that!' Jas couldn't believe what she was hearing.

Abby raised a hand. 'It'll be for your own good, Jas. If I can't stop you smoking, maybe Mum and Dad can. You know what they'll say. It'll be even worse than the time you dyed your hair green. Mum will go into orbit.'

Jas gritted her teeth and held her chin high. When she and Becky had had an accident with their hair, Mrs Scott had grounded her for ages. 'You're really mean, you know that?' she said quietly to Abby. 'I've told you, I'm not going to start smoking.'

'Good – then I won't have to say anything, will I?' Abby nodded at her meaningfully. 'And if you take my advice, you'll stop hanging round with Gina.'

'I can't do that, we're working on the fashion project together,' Jas wailed.

Abby shrugged. 'Well, just be careful, Jas.' And she went back to the sitting room.

Jas felt strangely angry – and a bit tearful, too. If she couldn't rely on her sister to understand, who could she trust? All the nagging and threats were enough to make someone *want* to smoke . . .

Oakwood Drive was one of the posh roads near the park. It was roughly halfway between Jas's house and Gina's. Isabel was already sitting on a wall by the postbox, waiting, when Jas arrived.

She'd taken special care to look good this morning, with her black leggings tucked into Chelsea boots and a black jeans jacket. Already, though, she was wishing she'd worn something lighter. It was a lovely day and if the sun kept shining, it was going to get hot.

'You look great,' Isabel commented as Jas approached. 'No one would guess you were just a second year. You look at least fifteen.'

'Thanks,' said Jas, feeling proud. 'You look nice too.'

Isabel blushed. She was wearing ordinary blue jeans and trainers, with a green sweater. Her straight shoulder-length dark hair was flecked with mahogany-coloured glints.

'Want a cigarette? No one will see us here.' She undid the cellophane wrapper from a fresh packet. 'One of the fifth-year girls bought them for me from the corner shop. She charged me an extra twenty pence, but it's worth it.'

Jas hesitated. After the way Abby had lectured her last night, she felt tempted to say yes. But she knew, deep-down, that Abby was right about smoking. It was just the way she'd gone on and on about it that had annoyed Jas.

'No, thanks.'

Isabel didn't argue. She helped herself to a cigarette and put the packet on the wall while she searched for a lighter. 'I know it's a bad habit,' she chattered as she tried her jeans pocket, 'but holding a cigarette makes me feel more confident. It gives you something to do with your hands, instead of just standing there.'

Jas suddenly became very aware of her hands dangling at her sides. She put one in her jacket pocket. But she could see what Isabel meant. You could pose with a cigarette. And it made Isabel look harder and more grown up.

'Aren't you worried about getting hooked?' Jas asked.

Isabel laughed. 'No way. I'll give it up when I'm sixteen. That's really cool, giving up when the others start.'

Jas shuffled her feet, impressed with Isabel's attitude. She was sorely tempted. A cigarette held casually in one hand would finish off her laid-back image perfectly. Smoking outdoors like this wouldn't make her clothes smell. And she'd just bought a whole new pack of gum she could chew to freshen her breath. There was no reason why she shouldn't get away with it.

'I've changed my mind,' she announced. 'Maybe I'll have one after all.' Isabel smiled and threw her the pack.

'Help yourself!' And she didn't laugh when Jas started coughing at her first puff.

They waited quietly for a few minutes. Jas was pleased it was Isabel she was with and not Vale or Gina. Isabel was much nicer. They talked about their outfits and the accessories they planned to buy.

'Gina's got a charge card for Peabody's,' Isabel confided, 'so we can get anything we want there.' She looked over Jas's shoulder. 'Is this Vale coming?'

Taking a puff on her cigarette, Jas turned – to see Liz Newman approaching, pushing a baby buggy. Holly, Liz's little sister, gave Jas a wave.

Panicking, Jas tried to hide the cigarette from Liz's sight. But in her hurry she dropped it and it lay smouldering on the ground. Jas would have put her foot on it if, at that second, the smoke hadn't caught the back of her throat and made her start coughing again.

Liz gave her a withering look as she walked by. 'I didn't know you'd started smoking,' she observed frostily. Holly leaned out of the buggy and tried to pick up the smouldering cigarette end, but Liz put her heel on it firmly. 'No, that's Jas's nasty cigarette,' she told Holly.

'Hi, Liz, hello, Holly,' Jas managed to gasp. 'Are you going to the park?' But Liz swept past, not bothering to stop.

'No!' Jas moaned, when she'd got her breath back and her eyes had stopped watering. 'Liz'll tell everyone.'

Isabel smiled sympathetically. 'Who cares what she thinks?' she asked. 'Liz is nice enough, but everything has to be perfect where she's concerned. She's always so organised and sensible about things—'

'She's kind and fun, too,' Jas inserted. Okay, Liz sometimes got on her nerves, but she was a good friend.

'And then there's Charlie always going on about animal rights and moaning at people who eat meat. I heard she told Marco Guillano off on Thursday for being cruel to his dog,' Isabel complained. 'She's so bossy.'

'Charlie loves animals,' Jas said, unwilling to hear her friend criticised, even though she felt the same way about Charlie sometimes.

'That's fine,' agreed Isabel, 'as long as she leaves other people to do their own thing. From what I hear, she told Marco that if he didn't look after his dog better, she'd call in the rescue squad from that animal shelter she goes to.'

'She works really hard there,' Jas insisted. 'The way some people treat their pets, I think it's a good thing there are people like Charlie around.'

'Well I don't think it's any of her business.' Isabel pulled out the cigarettes. 'And I don't think it matters what Liz Newman thinks of you.' She offered the cigarettes to Jas. 'Have another one. Don't let her dictate to you.'

Jas didn't really feel like smoking. Her throat still hurt from all the coughing. She watched Liz stop at the kerb and then push the buggy over the road. As she reached the far side, she turned back with another disapproving glance, as if to warn Jas – just as Abby had.

That did it. Jas reached for the pack. She wasn't going to let Liz tell her what she could and couldn't do.

'Have you got all the colours you want?' Gina asked, as they raided the fabric paints in Peabody's. 'There's a nice green shade here. And how about that yellow one?'

'They're really expensive,' Jas warned. 'I tried to buy some the other day.' Gina laughed and pulled a blue plastic card from her bag. 'I've got this, so we can charge anything we want.'

Jas felt a sudden thrill of excitement. Did this really mean they could choose anything? In that case, she'd have several more fabric paints, just in case.

'Jewellery, we need jewellery,' Gina decreed, leading them through the department. Jas was carrying

three bags containing ribbons and cotton and trim-
mings, the fabric paints, a straw sunhat and a pair of
emerald green cycle shorts that she'd spotted. They
might look good with her outfit, she'd wondered –
so Gina had just grabbed them, no questions asked.
It was amazing!

'What about this?' Isabel was holding up some
dangling silver earrings with tiny bells on the ends.

'Not for me,' Jas said, giggling. 'Aren't there any
earrings with a bucket and spade on them?' She
moved up the counter to where the necklaces and
bangles were.

Her eyes fell on a bangle covered in shells. It
would look great with her outfit – and it wasn't too
expensive. 'Gina!' she called – and saw the matching
necklace on the rack. It was gorgeous, strand after
strand of tiny shells with larger ones threaded on. It
would look absolutely amazing with her shell-strewn
outfit.

'It's expensive,' she warned, as Gina examined it.
More than she'd ever dream of paying for a necklace
herself.

'It's lovely, though.' Gina handed it to the sales
assistant. 'We'll have it.'

Jas could hardly believe it. Nor could she wipe the
huge smile off her face. It was so exciting!

Next stop was the shoe department, where Gina
bought a pair of gold pumps and Vale had a pair of
red, white and blue baseball boots. Jas was tempted
by a pair of sand-coloured suede loafers with a shell
design on the cross-bar, but they didn't have her size.

'Tough,' commiserated Gina, handing Vale the
shoes to carry. 'We can come back next week and

try again. Now let's go to the toy store and get Isabel a bucket and spade,' she suggested. 'And maybe they'll have a stars and stripes flag for Vale, too.'

Giggling, Isabel grabbed Jas's hand and pulled her through the crowds of shoppers. Jas hadn't had such fun for ages. She smiled across at Gina, leading the way. Maybe she wasn't such a difficult person to get along with after all!

The four of them hurried along the crowded mall, looking into windows as they went. 'Hey!' Vale stopped outside the charity store that had opened a few weeks ago selling second-hand clothing.

'We don't want to buy old things,' protested Gina, looking shocked.

'I know,' laughed Vale, pointing. 'But look who does!'

Jas followed the direction of her finger – and saw Emma and Charlie flicking through the racks of clothes. Emma pulled out an old-fashioned dress and held it up, while Charlie assessed it.

'Aren't you glad you're not still in their team?' Isabel chuckled. 'What *do* they think they're doing?'

'I don't know. Probably one of Charlie's weird ideas.' Jas shook her head. Isabel was right. Thank goodness she was in Gina's team!

'More mango sorbet?' Mrs Galloway asked, pointing to the crystal bowl of dessert. 'Or some Camembert? It's nice and ripe.'

'No thank you,' said Jas, eyeing the cheese. She could smell it from across the table. If she actually had to *eat* it she'd be sick.

'That was a lovely lunch, Mummy,' Gina said,

throwing her napkin down on the table. They were eating in the sun-filled conservatory of the Galloway's house. Jas had never seen anything like it before. It was full of tropical plants and overhead grew a vine with real grapes hanging in bunches.

And she'd never had food like it before, either. Usually when she ate at her friends' houses they had everyday food – pizza, or salad or chicken. But Mrs Galloway had made a quiche with smoked salmon and asparagus, which seemed pretty unusual. That had been nice, but the salad tasted bitter and was full of leaves Jas didn't recognise. She'd left most of it. To be honest, she'd have preferred pizza in front of the TV, or beans on toast.

Mrs Galloway smiled. 'I know you want to run upstairs to look through all the things you bought this morning. Off you go.'

Gina pushed her chair back and Jas got up with relief. Did the Galloways eat like this every day?

It would be worth putting up with lunch, she decided as they unpacked the shoes and jewellery, if she could have all these things. She tried on the green cycle shorts and draped the sand-coloured silk over them.

'When you've finished your top, it'll look brilliant,' Isabel assured her. 'Kind of fun and elegant at the same time.' Jas felt thrilled. Her outfit was going to be simply amazing – once Mrs Harper had done her bit, of course.

Gina had opened the bag of jewellery and was admiring the shell necklace. 'This is just beautiful, isn't it?' she asked, going over to her dressing table so she could inspect herself in the mirror.

'It's the best necklace I've ever seen,' agreed Jas, itching to get her hands on it. She could just see herself in it now.

'I was thinking . . .' The cunning gleam that Jas was learning to be wary of reappeared in Gina's silver eyes. 'This necklace would look really great with my top. I mean,' she added before Jas could interject, 'my outfit's quite exotic and so is this.' She stroked the strings of tiny shells. 'I expect a lot of these shells came from the Caribbean in the first place, so it's just perfect for me.'

'But it was for *me*.' Jas frowned. 'It's ideal for my outfit. That was why I chose it. If I hadn't seen it, you'd never have bought it.'

Gina smiled sweetly at her. 'I know, and it was really clever of you to see how lovely it was. That's why I wanted you on my team, Jas. I knew you'd have good ideas.'

Jas took a deep breath. Did Gina think she could soft-soap her into forgetting that the necklace had been intended for her?

Isabel came over, carrying the plastic bucket and spade they'd bought. 'There were other necklaces like that one,' she told them. 'You could get another.'

Gina shook her head. 'That's no good. We don't all want to wear the same things, do we?' She stared at herself in the mirror, pouting at her reflection. 'No, I think it's best if I keep this and Jas finds something else for herself.'

Jas glowered – but what could she say? Gina had bought the necklace, after all. Jas couldn't really complain. It was a mean thing to do, all the same, promising her something and then snatching it away again. But she should have expected it all along, she supposed.

Vale was mooching around in her new baseball boots. 'What are we going to do?' she asked. 'Until Mrs Harper's cut the bits out for us, we can't start making our designs up.'

Gina took off the shell necklace, opened a drawer in the dressing table and put it carefully inside. 'I guess we can dismiss now, but we ought to get together next week and start work on the sewing and fabric-painting. Tuesday after school?'

Vale grinned. 'That gives us ten days to get everything done. It'll be easy!'

Jas wished she could believe it. But in her present mood she felt sure that the next couple of weeks were going to be anything but easy . . .

Gina was just jealous, Jas reasoned as she walked home chewing on two sticks of gum. Gina knew that with that gorgeous shell necklace Jas's outfit would be perfect – and of course, Gina couldn't bear that. There was only going to be one star of the show – Gina Galloway herself.

Jas kicked a stone and it bounced into the road. She wished it had been Gina's head.

And to make things worse, Stuart's motorbike was parked in the drive when Jas got back to her own house. That was all she needed. She breathed into her cupped hands before she went in. Her breath didn't smell of cigarette smoke to her, just mint.

There was no one inside, but the patio doors in the dining-room were open and Jas could see her mum stretched out on a sun lounger, enjoying the weather. The breeze blew a gust of charcoal smoke into the house.

'You didn't tell me you were going to have a barbecue!' Jas accused as she went out. Her father was standing over the grill, wearing shorts and a full-length apron.

'I didn't realise we had to discuss everything with you before we went ahead,' he laughed. He was tall and dark-haired, but going silvery at the sides of his head.

'Did you have lunch with your friends?' Mrs Scott asked.

'Sort of.' Jas stared at the few chicken legs and ribs charring nicely on the barbecue. 'But there wasn't much of it. Have you got anything going spare?'

Her mother smiled. 'Abby and Stuart are in the kitchen getting some more chicken and sausages. They came home unexpectedly. Go and tell them what you want.'

Jas squinted up at the sun. 'And maybe I'll change into my swimsuit and get some sun while I'm waiting for it to cook.'

'Bring the sun block,' called her mother as she went into the kitchen.

Abby and Stuart, who'd been having a cuddle, moved hurriedly apart. Abby blushed. 'I thought you were out with your friends?'

'I was, but now I'm back. And I'd like two chicken legs, please,' Jas said simply, determined not to get into another fight.

'How about these?' offered Stuart, putting two uncooked ones on a plate for her. 'That Miss Tyler

88

was very nice when I saw her in school. Not the dragon you warned me about.'

'You obviously got her on a good day,' Jas said coolly. 'Put them on the barbecue for me, will you? I want to go and change.'

'Hold on a second.' Abby came over from the sink. She stood on tiptoe and began to sniff Jas, starting with the top of her head and moving down.

'What are you doing?' Jas protested.

'Smoke detection,' Abby said with a stern expression. 'Remember what I told you yesterday?'

Abby took another sniff round her shoulders. 'I can definitely smell something,' she announced. 'Have you been smoking again?'

Jas sighed deeply, as if her big sister was totally mad. 'If I smell smoky it's because I've just been standing out there by the barbie, talking to Dad,' she said slowly, as if she were talking to someone really stupid. 'I don't know what's got into you, Abby. You're so suspicious!'

Abby drew back. 'I'm just keeping an eye on you,' she protested.

'I know,' Jas called back over her shoulder as she went upstairs, smiling to herself. *But you're not going to catch me out,* she thought.

7

'Can you show me how to turn up this hem? I can't do it properly.' Gina looked up at Jas with a syrupy-sweet smile. 'You did the hem of your top really neatly.' She was sitting at the sewing machine in the linen room at the Galloway's home.

Jas gritted her teeth. 'I had to do it by hand, remember? You and Vale were hogging the machine,' she reminded Gina.

The last week had been a nightmare. First of all, Mrs Harper had taken ages to get all the outfits cut out. It wasn't till Wednesday that Jas had been able to start sewing hers together. And then on Thursday Gina had announced that she was busy and they couldn't come round and use the sewing machine. Today was Saturday, and Jas still had to finish painting the design on the sand-coloured silk *and* sew shells on it.

'Please, Jas?' Gina fluttered her eyelashes. 'You're so good at this kind of thing.'

'All right,' Jas said with a sigh. Experience had taught her that it was quicker to do what Gina said, rather than argue about it. She sat down on the stool that Gina had just vacated. 'All you do is turn the fabric over like this, and then . . .' She

turned her head to make sure Gina was watching –
but Gina was disappearing through the linen room
doorway.

'Hey!' Jas called. But Gina didn't stop.

'I'll leave you to it. I know you'll make a good
job of it,' she purred. 'Vale's bought some new
make-up and we're going to try it on.' And the
door shut firmly behind her.

Jas felt like Cinderella – a feeling she was getting
more and more used to. Vale and Gina always
managed to exclude her from their plans. They
behaved pretty much the same way towards Isabel,
but Isabel didn't get wound up about it the way
Jas did. She just stayed away, like she had this
morning.

It took Jas half an hour to finish off the hem of
Gina's wrap-round skirt with its thigh-high slit. When
she returned to Gina's room, Gina and Vale were
in the bathroom, trying on make-up in front of the
mirror.

Gina's bathroom was decorated in a peach colour,
with flowery tiles and thick towels to match. All the
taps and fittings were shiny gold. 'I wanted a Jacuzzi,'
she'd confided in Jas, 'but my parents said no. Still, I
can always use theirs if I want to.'

'What do you think?' asked Vale, turning round
as Jas came in. She shut her eyes and revealed blue
eyelids with white stars dotted over them.

It looked pretty awful to Jas – but then she felt
that way about Vale's outfit in general. It just wasn't
her style.

'It'll certainly make people look at you,' she
giggled.

91

'It's making my eyes itch, too,' complained Vale. She began to rub them. 'Maybe the stars aren't such a good idea.'

'Here's your skirt, Gina.' Jas threw it over the towel rack.

Gina didn't bother to look. 'I heard that Mina and her team are just doing ordinary shorts and T-shirt outfits,' she said. 'And apparently one of the teams from 3C are wearing macs and wet suits – it's supposed to be a witty comment on English summer weather.'

'Sounds more like fancy dress than fashion to me,' said Vale, taking her make-up off with Gina's cleansing lotion and a huge wad of cotton wool.

'They won't even get a look-in,' Gina said confidently as she checked her appearance in the mirror. 'This is great with my Caribbean outfit, don't you think?'

She held a lighted cigarette in one hand while she applied a grape-coloured lipstick with the other. Her eyes were already surrounded by smudges of purple shadow that picked up some of the moodier shades in the fabric.

Jas almost burst out laughing! With her pale skin and dark eyes and lips, Gina looked like she was auditioning to be a member of the Addams Family! 'Perhaps some brighter colours would look better,' she suggested.

There was a palette of eye colours by the basin, including a gorgeous gold shade. By the side of it lay a tub of bronzer, with a fluffy blusher brush. Jas reached across for them. Some bronzer across her cheekbones would give her a healthy glow. And the gold eyeshadow would look great if she used it carefully.

Gina's hand descended on hers before she could pick the cosmetics up. 'I'm using that to give me a Caribbean bronzed look,' she said sharply.

'Can't I use it too?' Jas asked, amazed. Nothing could ever make Gina, with her skin as white as fresh milk, look bronzed!

'I don't like sharing make-up,' Gina said tartly. 'It's unhygienic.'

Jas blinked her eyes disbelievingly. 'I've seen you try Vale's lip gloss.'

'That was Vale's, and she doesn't mind sharing – but *I* do,' insisted Gina, fluffing up her hair until it floated round her head like a cloud.

'I'll try that, then.' Jas had spotted an eyeshadow compact still in its brand new box.

But Gina snatched it up. 'Actually,' she said with the kind of steel edge to her voice that Jas was beginning to know well, 'Vale and I have got to go now.'

'I thought we were going to spend the day finishing off our outfits?' Jas was bewildered. Just yesterday, Gina had urged her to come over early so they could get lots of work done. Now she was intending to give up halfway through the morning. What was she playing at?

'I don't feel like sitting indoors sewing when it's sunny outside,' Gina complained. 'And neither does Vale. So we've decided to go riding. Jasper needs some exercise. I haven't taken him out for a gallop for nearly two weeks.'

Jasper was Gina's pony, and Vale had her own horse at the same stables. Jas had never seen Jasper, but from all accounts he was as mean-tempered as Gina herself. She'd once planned to bring him to the school fête and give pony rides – until Miss Tyler heard that he liked biting people!

'When are you going to get your outfits finished?' Jas asked, feeling worried. If Vale and Gina didn't get down to work, they wouldn't be ready for Friday's fashion show. They could hardly go swanning down the catwalk with their outfits held together with pins, could they?

'Mrs Harper can always give us a hand,' Gina said nonchalantly, walking into her dressing room and pulling her jodhpurs and riding boots from one of the cupboards. 'If you're worried, you can take your outfit home with you, Jas, and finish it off there.'

She threw Jas a bag to put the sand-coloured silk top into. 'I'll give you a hand,' offered Vale, who'd been disposing of the cigarette ends down the loo. She helped Jas pack up the fabric paints and all the other things she'd need. Jas felt as if she'd been dismissed and Gina wanted her out of the house as soon as possible.

Vale ushered her down the stairs. 'I've got to go home and get my riding kit,' she called as she went up the next-door drive. 'See you at school on Monday!'

'Listen, everyone!' Miss Tyler glared at her students through her red-rimmed glasses. Red was Miss Tyler's favourite colour, and today she was wearing cherry red trousers and a crisp white blouse with red stitching.

'Come on, settle down,' she called, getting out the register. 'Ryan Bryson, get down off that window sill and sit at your desk.'

Jas sighed. It was Monday morning, and on Monday mornings everyone wanted to talk about what they'd been doing at the weekend. Everyone except her. For one thing, there was no one for her to talk to. Liz was still casting her dirty looks and muttering to Becky – all about seeing her smoking, no doubt. And for another, she'd had such a boring weekend, there was nothing to talk about.

Before Miss Tyler could call the register, the classroom door opened and Charlie came in. She looked pale and near to tears – which for Charlie was really something. Jas had often seen Charlie angry, but she rarely cried.

'Are you okay?' she asked, concerned, as Charlie brushed past her desk.

'Mmm,' Charlie murmured unconvincingly. Something had happened, Jas felt sure. She turned round and saw Liz and Becky questioning Charlie, but Charlie didn't seem to be saying much to them, either.

'What's going on?' Jas whispered to Mina. She was itching to know. Since splitting up with her friends, she'd felt starved of gossip.

'I don't know,' Mina shrugged. 'Maybe she had another fight with Marco. She doesn't like the way he treats his dog.'

Jas remembered what Isabel had said about Charlie and Marco. Marco was a fourth-year. He sometimes brought his dog to school and he and his friends showed off, making it do tricks and teasing it. Charlie always went wild when she saw what was happening but till now she'd always steered clear of doing or saying anything.

But there wasn't time to think about that now. 'Fashion show!' Miss Tyler bellowed above the noise. The chatter stopped. 'Thank you,' she said with a tight smile. 'Now, how many of you have made outfits for the fashion show?'

Sixteen hands shot up. 'Will you please bring your outfits into school on Wednesday,' Miss Tyler instructed. 'At lunchtime there will be a special meeting in this room so that we can iron out any problems with the things you've made.'

'You can't iron mine,' interrupted Ryan. 'It's made of plastic.'

Miss Tyler shot him a pained look. 'I can't wait to see – and that goes for all of you. I'm looking forward to seeing how creative you've all been. Once I know what you're planning to wear, I can decide on an order for the fashion show and give you some information about what to do on the day. So Wednesday lunchtime, everyone. Don't forget.'

Almost as soon as Miss Tyler had finished speaking, something stung Jas on the back of the neck. She looked down to see a paper pellet on the desk in front of her. 'Who did that?' She turned, accusingly. Gina was waving a ruler at her.

'See you at my house tomorrow, to finish everything,' she mouthed.

'Mine's finished – I don't need to come.' Jas was still feeling sore about Saturday morning. She wasn't going to be at Gina's beck and call any more, now her outfit was done.

And it was worth all the hassle, she decided, thinking of it hanging in her wardrobe at home. The top looked great. Even Abby had admired it when she'd come in looking for some earrings. Jas could hardly believe she'd created anything so nice. It was partly due to Gina's mum, of course, for letting her have the fabric. But it was Jas's idea that really counted.

She looked wistfully across at Becky and Liz and Charlie, wishing she could show it to them and prove how wrong they'd been to laugh at it. But they'd see on Wednesday, anyway.

Another pellet came whistling across the room and grazed the top of her head. 'What now?' Jas demanded, rubbing the spot.

'We need to rehearse,' Gina hissed at her. 'We've got to get together and make sure all the details are right. All four of us *have* to be there.'

'All right!' Jas sighed. She supposed Gina did have a point. They needed to practise modelling their outfits so that on Friday they could walk away with first prize. And Jas felt sure they would. Their designs were bound to be the best – and of the four in their team, hers was the best of all!

'Is my dress okay? It feels a bit big.' Isabel inspected herself in front of the full-length mirror in Gina's room.

'It's fine,' Jas reassured her. She liked Isabel's dress. It had a Sixties look to it, and Isabel had tied her hair up in bunches to go with the style. She carried a red plastic bucket as a handbag. 'It looks really great,' said Jas.

'Yours does, too,' said Isabel.

Jas twirled in front of the mirror. Her outfit, as unlikely as it had looked on paper, had worked perfectly. The silk hung down in swingy folds just as she'd imagined it would, and the splodgy multi-coloured pattern of seashells and starfish looked great. Last night, as a finishing touch, she'd glued some of her seashell collection on to the crossbars of an old pair of loafers, and stuck more shells on a pair of old earrings her mother didn't want. They finished the outfit off perfectly. It wasn't the kind of thing you'd wear every day, as Liz had pointed out. But it was original and unusual and Jas loved wearing it.

'Here we come!' Gina called as she and Vale emerged from the bedroom to admire themselves in the mirror. Gina's outfit had been finished very quickly. The halter top and skirt were pretty, but on Gina, with her pale colouring and boney shoulders, they weren't quite right. And though she'd tied a scarf round her hair, it still bobbed about in its usual fashion, as if it might float off on its own at any moment.

Vale's outfit featured preppie-style red and white striped walking shorts. They were a bit tight and made her walk as if she was desperate to go to the loo. 'You'll just have to lose weight,' instructed Gina.

'But it's only three days to go!' Vale protested.

'Then don't eat,' Gina snapped. Jas was pleased to see that Vale had decided to leave off the fancy eye make-up. With her red, white and blue base-ball boots, the star-patterned top and matching red cheeks, she looked unusual, but okay.

'Will you be holding a cigarette as you go down

the catwalk?' Jas asked laughingly, referring to the one Vale was clutching.

'Can you imagine what Miss Tyler and Wiggy would have to say?' Vale grinned, pretending she was on stage and taking a drag. Isabel and Jas giggled.

'We'll practise walking up and down,' Gina announced stonily. 'I'm the team leader, so I'll go first, then Vale, then Isabel and Jas last.'

Jas almost laughed. She might have guessed Gina would want her at the back!

Gina set off across her bedroom, trying to look elegant. 'When you get to the bottom of the catwalk, you have to turn round like this. My mother showed me. It's what professional models do.'

She did some fancy footwork, turned on the spot, caught one of her high heels in the bedside rug and fell flat on her face. 'Are we all supposed to do that?' Vale asked sarcastically.

Gina's face was nearly as red as her friend's. 'It was just an accident,' she muttered, straightening the halter-necked top, which was almost strangling her. 'If any of you do that on Friday, I'll kill you,' she warned. She sashayed across the bedroom once more, carefully avoiding the rug.

Jas stifled a giggle. Gina could totter around on heels like a bimbo if she wanted to, but *she* was going to bounce down the catwalk. Her outfit was for having fun in. 'Will there be music?' she asked.

'I think so,' said Isabel. 'We could dance down the stage.' And she and Jas waltzed across the bedroom, laughing. Jas felt so good. She couldn't wait for

Friday, when she could show her design off to the school.

Gina was frowning when they turned round. And she kept frowning for the next half hour, as they discussed all the details of the show.

'I've been thinking,' she announced at last, when they'd run through everything they'd need. She fixed her silvery grey eyes on Jas. 'Your outfit would look really great on me.'

Jas was puzzled. 'But it's mine.' She laughed and took a puff of the cigarette Isabel had given her.

'But the colours would look better on me than they do on you,' Gina said firmly, as if there was no reason why Jas should argue back. 'And you'd look good in the bright colours of my outfit.'

'But I made this for *me*,' Jas responded, stroking the silk as she glanced at the other two. They both looked away quickly.

'Maybe, but you made it using my fabric, on my sewing machine,' Gina said with a reptilian smile. 'In a way, you could say that outfit's mine already. You just happen to be wearing it.'

Jas blanched. Was Gina serious? 'I designed it,' she said defensively, 'and I'm going to wear it on Friday.'

'In that case you'll be in a team of one.' Gina stood up. 'Because unless you agree to swap outfits, you're not going to be in my team.'

Jas laughed angrily. 'Well if I'm out of your team, then the whole team's out of the contest. Or have you forgotten that you need four people?'

'There's Lucy Groves and Pritti Saldhana and loads of other people who'd jump at the chance of joining my team.' Gina looked incredibly calm and serious. Jas began to realise just how calculating she was.

'They wouldn't have time to produce a design,' Jas argued.

'I wouldn't bet on it. We've got everything they need right here,' Gina replied. She'd thought of everything, Jas realised.

'Why not just swap outfits instead of making such a fuss?' Vale joined in. 'They're going to be judging us as a team. If Gina looks better in your outfit, and you look good in hers, then it does the team a favour, doesn't it?'

'You're just jealous,' Jas said. 'My outfit's the best, so Gina wants to wear it.'

'Don't be stupid! It's got nothing to do with jealousy,' Gina protested, looking incredibly innocent. 'It's for the sake of the team, that's all. You've got to do it, Jas.'

Jas looked at Isabel for support, but Isabel just shrugged. 'It might be for the best, you know,' she murmured. Jas felt sure there was a hint of sympathy in her eyes.

She felt trapped. If she wanted to get through this round of the fashion show, she had no choice but to stick with Gina. After that, Gina had better watch out. No way could she pretend that the sand-coloured top was her own idea. She'd have to give it back so that Jas could wear it.

'Do I take it you're willing to swap?' Gina asked quietly.

'You're a mean cheat,' Jas protested. 'I should have known better than to get into the same team as you.'

'But you've got no alternative, have you?' Gina didn't bother to hide her pleasure. 'So that's settled then. On Friday, I'll wear Jas's outfit and she'll appear in my Caribbean holiday gear.' And she smiled her horrible, smug smile . . .

8

'I didn't know that Jamie Thompson had joined up with Ryan and Sean,' Jas said, looking at the crowd of kids bustling round the classroom on Wednesday lunchtime. It was so crowded, lots of people had to wait outside the door.

They were all carrying bags and, in some cases, huge boxes, with tantalising bits and pieces sticking out.

Ryan and Sean went by with a pile of black plastic. Jamie and another boy followed behind with what looked like a length of drainpipe. Jas's mind boggled as she wondered what they could possibly be planning.

'I heard there were nearly forty teams entering in all,' Isabel announced. She stared round the room. 'Vale and Gina are over there.'

Jas reluctantly joined them. She could hardly bear to be with Gina since she'd pulled that stunt the other night. At the moment Jas just wished she could disappear from Wetherton and make a new life somewhere else.

'Unpack your outfits and lay them out on the desks,' Miss Tyler instructed. 'I'm just going to come round to see what you've made. If you're having any problems, we'll try and solve them. Once I've seen your outfits, you can leave them here. I'll put them in a safe place till Friday.'

Jas pulled the multi-coloured halter-necked outfit from her bag and smoothed it out on the desk. Gina, with a smug smile, took the sand-coloured silk top out of a large green and gold Harrods carrier bag. It was just like Gina, Jas thought, to bring the outfit to school in a bag from a posh London store.

'While you're doing that, I'll just give you some details of the fashion show itself,' Miss Tyler continued. 'It's going to be held after school on Friday. You'll be able to change into your outfits in the gym changing rooms. I'll give you a number tomorrow, which is the order you'll be appearing on stage.'

'Will there be music?' asked Jas.

'Yes. Mr Harris is in charge of the music and he's going to give us a mixture of tracks,' Miss Tyler said. 'The drama club are going to create a catwalk, and you can walk or dance down it.'

'Who are the judges?' Ryan wanted to know.

'Myself, Mr Leach and Miss Diamond from the art department.' Miss Tyler raised her red pen. 'I'll be on stage, with a microphone, to announce each team and tell everyone your names. If you want to give me details of your outfits, I can tell the audience about them.'

'It sounds pretty professional,' murmured Isabel. 'Miss Tyler's obviously got everything under control.' She held up her dress. ' "And here we have Isabel, modelling a charming little dress, perfect for an evening at the disco after a day on the beach," ' she said in a posh voice and made Jas laugh.

They spread their garments out over a couple

of desks. On one side, Mina Chotai's team were laying out coordinating shorts and vest tops. On the other, some first-years were getting outfits made out of old beach towels ready.

Gina giggled dismissively. 'So much for the competition! If this is the best they can do, we're going to walk away with the prize.'

'I don't know. Look over there,' said Vale. 'Have you seen what Liz Newman's team's been up to?'

Jas turned to look. Miss Tyler was laughing as Becky held up her outfit – which seemed to be a short shift dress covered in paper fringes made from the colourful front pages of holiday brochures. Jas felt a twinge of surprise. It was a clever idea – and the way Becky had done it, it looked great, too. She'd even made a matching paper hat from a brochure.

'She's just stapled them on to the dress or something!' grumbled Vale. 'I reckon that's cheating.'

Jas couldn't help smiling. Becky had said how much she hated sewing – and she'd found an easy way out of it.

But Miss Tyler didn't seem to think there was any cheating involved. 'Very imaginative,' she said with a laugh. 'And you too, Charlie. I thought you might try something a bit different.'

Charlie's outfit was made of recycled bits and pieces. There was a very long item a bit like a skirt. It was made out of lots of overlapping pieces of clear plastic, shaped to look like fish scales and stapled together. Lots of kids crowded round Miss Tyler to take a look at it.

'Oooh,' said Mina to one of her team-mates, 'I wish we'd thought of something like that.'

'When I'm wearing it, it looks a bit like a mermaid's tail,' Charlie explained. 'It sort of fans out behind me.' For the top she'd made a mermaid's bra with two large flat shells and some ribbons and string. There was also an amazing hat with bits of driftwood.

'It could be a bit revealing,' Miss Tyler said dubiously.

Charlie and Liz roared with laughter. 'I'm going to wear a leotard and leggings underneath,' Charlie explained, blushing. 'Otherwise it's see-through.'

Miss Tyler looked relieved. 'Actually,' Liz added, 'we liked Charlie's outfit so much we thought we'd call our team the Mermaids. Could you say that when you introduce us?'

Jas was feeling more and more surprised by the second. How come Becky and Charlie had suddenly developed such great ideas? More than ever, she wished that she'd stuck with them. Her outfit would have looked so good with theirs . . . It made her want to cry.

'If they're going to call themselves the Mermaids, we're going to be the Millionaires,' Gina announced, tossing her head so that her hair threatened to fly off across the classroom. She was obviously furious. 'Millionaires are a million times better than mermaids.'

She got even more furious when Liz and Emma showed Miss Tyler their designs. Emma's was an old-fashioned bathing suit, with knee-length pantaloons and a baggy top. She also had a parasol and sun hat. Miss Tyler was examining it closely. 'It started off as a trouser suit from the charity shop,' Emma explained. 'I just chopped it up a bit.'

106

'That's *got* to be cheating!' Vale declared in a quiet voice.

Gina spoke up. 'Don't you think that's cheating?' she asked Miss Tyler. 'Our team have made all our outfits ourselves.'

Miss Tyler shrugged. 'There's nothing in the rules against adapting an outfit. You couldn't just buy something and wear it as it is, of course. But Emma's done a lot of work on this.'

'It's favouritism,' Gina fumed to her team. 'Miss Tyler's always being soft on that lot.'

Liz's outfit was just as witty as Becky's and Charlie's. 'It's based on the idea of a picnic,' she explained, 'because when my family go on holiday we always have picnics.'

She'd taken an old checked tablecloth and cut a hole in the middle to make a skirt. Like Charlie, she'd made a kind of bra top with paper plates. On each of them were stuck chunky sandwiches and an apple.

'You've made them out of papier mâché,' exclaimed Miss Tyler, prodding the food with her finger.

'I'll be wearing a leotard underneath, like Charlie,' Liz explained. 'And I've got a necklace made out of plastic cutlery.' She held it up. 'And a hat, too . . .'

Jas couldn't believe it. What had Liz said to her about *her* outfit not being suitable for everyday? Was Liz intending to wear a tablecloth from now on? But even though she felt a bit annoyed about Liz's change of plan, Jas couldn't help acknowledging that the outfit looked like great fun. And it must have been really great, finding all the bits to make them. Oh, why had she been so quick to swap sides?

Miss Tyler smiled warmly and jotted down a few details on her notepad. 'Right, girls, you can put your outfits on my desk and I'll keep them safe till Friday.'

The four Mermaids grinned at each other jubilantly as they gathered their things up. Miss Tyler moved on to Sean and Ryan's team. 'Our outfits are for a holiday on the Moon,' Ryan explained.

'What a stupid idea,' Gina sneered, turning away. 'It seems to me that we're the only team who've produced *proper* fashionable outfits. The others are all silly gimmicks.'

'No they're not,' protested Mina, pointing to her team's matching shorts and vests. 'Look at ours.'

'Yours are just *boring*,' Gina said with a yawn.

'Get lost,' Mina responded spiritedly.

Jas turned away from the lot of them. She was sick of Gina's squabbling. And she could also feel her confidence wavering a bit. Some of the other teams' outfits were surprisingly good. Especially the Mermaids'.

'We're the Millionaires team,' Vale told Miss Tyler when she arrived at their outfits. 'Could you say that when you announce us?'

'Why are you calling yourself the Millionaires?' Miss Tyler asked, raising one eyebrow above her red-rimmed spectacles.

'Because our team's theme is holidays around the world to exotic places and you have to be rich to travel,' Gina improvised. 'Vale's theme is New York, for example, and this one – ' she pointed to the halter-neck top, '– is for a Caribbean holiday.'

Jas and Isabel looked at each other questioningly.

Where did *their* outfits fit into this theme?

'Right,' Miss Tyler nodded, jotting the details down, her red pen flying over the page. 'This is lovely,' she added appreciatively, reaching out to touch the silky sand-coloured top. 'The painting on this is beautiful. Gosh, it's real silk!' She was obviously impressed.

'It's mine,' snapped Gina, with a warning stare at Jas.

'It was my idea,' Jas insisted on saying. 'And I painted it.'

'You did a beautiful job.' Miss Tyler had moved on to Vale's shorts and top and Isabel's dress. 'They're nicely made,' she commented. 'Obviously no expense was spared.' She passed over the multi-coloured halter-neck top with barely a glance.

Jas's heart sank as she watched Miss Tyler scribbling down some notes on her pad. No one was going to notice the halter-neck top and split skirt when they had moon monsters and mermaids and picnic outfits to goggle at. At this rate, the fashion show was going to be a disaster for her.

'We interpreted the rules of the competition properly,' Gina went on. 'We've made proper outfits, from scratch – we didn't go out and buy them.'

Miss Tyler looked at her coolly. 'I've already told you, Gina, that I don't regard Emma's outfit as cheating. Not everyone has the money or facilities to buy beautiful fabrics and make clothes from scratch. As far as I'm concerned, imagination is worth just as much as hard cash.'

Two red spots of rage appeared on Gina's white cheeks as their teacher moved on down the aisle.

'Tyler's got it in for me,' she hissed. 'She's never liked me – just because my parents have got money! It's not fair.'

Jas, placing her outfit on the pile on Miss Tyler's desk, thought that Gina was probably correct. Miss Tyler probably did think Gina was a rich, spoiled brat with all the advantages. And she was right!

Jas finished packing her pencils and stuffed them in her bag. As she did so, a piece of multi-coloured fabric caught her eye. It was the sash that went round the waist of the halter-neck outfit. 'Bum,' she muttered. She'd better take it down to Miss Tyler, otherwise it might get lost.

As she emerged from the classroom, holding the sash, she ran straight into Becky and Liz. For the last few days they'd managed to steer well clear of each other. Jas had developed a kind of radar that told her when they were around. When she caught a glimpse of them, she kept well away. But now there was no escape. They couldn't pretend they hadn't noticed each other.

'Hi,' Jas mumbled, feeling her ears burn with embarrassment.

'Hi.' They both looked wary, but not unfriendly.

'I really liked your outfits,' Jas blurted. 'They were so different from the ones you planned originally.'

Liz gave a gentle smile. 'Well, we decided that you were right when you said we needed to make our designs fun, not practical.'

Jas swallowed hard. It somehow made her feel even worse to know that *she'd* been the one to spark off their ideas.

'And I liked your idea of giving the team a name. The Mermaids – it's nice,' she added.

'Yeah, we thought so.' There was an arrogant sparkle in Becky's bright blue eyes. 'We remembered what you'd said about using a mermaid design on your outfit, you see. And mermaids are pretty magical and special, so we thought it would be a good team name.'

Jas nodded. 'So I was responsible for *that* idea too, was I?' she said. There was an edge in her voice.

Liz rolled her eyes long-sufferingly. 'Let's not get into another fight, please.' She hauled her school bag, packed with neat, colour-coordinated files, over her shoulder. 'I said I'd meet Josh in the playground. See you.'

'I'll come with you,' said Becky. The two of them walked quickly away down the corridor, leaving Jas feeling thoroughly put down. But, she reflected as she followed them from a safe distance, they had every right to be arrogant. From being losers, they'd turned the tables – and looked like being winners.

Miss Tyler was in the Technology workshop, fixing a new bit into one of the drills. She looked up as Jas knocked and came in.

'I left this off my outfit,' Jas explained, handing the sash over. 'Could you take it for me? Otherwise I'll probably forget to bring it on Friday.'

'Of course.' Miss Tyler smiled. 'I'll put it away in a minute.' She glanced over her shoulder towards the walk-in storeroom where some of the CDT materials were kept. Students weren't allowed in it without a teacher's permission. 'I think there's room to squeeze this in,' she said, laughing. 'Don't worry about a thing, Jas. All the outfits are safe till Friday!'

'I really liked Charlie's outfit,' Gina enthused as she walked down the school drive by Jas's side. Vale walked on the other. Jas, who'd been heading home on her own when they'd caught up with her, felt as if she was under a police escort.

'Of course,' Gina wittered on, 'I'm not really surprised by how imaginative it is. Charlie's always been so arty. But I'd really like to take a closer look at it and see how she made it.'

Jas darted a sceptical glance at Gina. At lunchtime she'd been furious about Charlie's recycled mermaid outfit. Why had Gina changed her tune so suddenly?

'We'll see all the outfits again soon enough, on Friday,' Jas said flatly.

Gina smiled. 'Yes, you're right,' she agreed.

There was a pause, then Vale asked casually, 'I wonder where Miss Tyler's keeping the outfits? I thought she might put them in the cupboards in the craft room, but she'll need more space than that.'

'I think they're in the CDT storeroom,' Jas responded without thinking.

'Oh,' said Vale, not seeming to take much notice.

Jas just wished the pair of them would go away and leave her alone. She'd had more of them than she could take.

'Here.' As they came to the end of the school drive, Gina fished into her black leather duffle bag – the one that had cost nearly a hundred pounds, according to her – and secretively pulled out a long, slender packet of cigarettes. 'Have one of these,' she murmured, sticking a cigarette into the top pocket of Jas's jeans jacket.

Jas tried to get it out. 'I don't want it,' she protested.

'You should be grateful,' Gina scolded. 'They're the most expensive cigarettes you can buy. My mum bought some for a friend of hers when she went to London yesterday – and I managed to get hold of a packet.' She chuckled. 'Save it for when you really want a smoke.'

Jas was still fiddling around. The cigarette had got stuck at the bottom of her pocket and she couldn't get it out. 'I honestly don't want it,' she insisted, glaring murderously at Gina. Her glance also fell on Liz and Charlie coming towards them down the drive and casting suspicious looks in her direction. She didn't want them to see her exchanging cigarettes with Gina in broad daylight. 'Okay,' she said, patting the pocket and turning quickly away. 'I'll see you, Gina.'

'Bye, Jas.' Gina stood at the end of the drive, waving and smiling as if she were Jas's best friend.

Jas was still seething when she got home. The house was quiet. She helped herself to a can of Coke and a couple of biscuits, then went upstairs to her room. There was some geography homework she had to complete for tomorrow, and an English essay, too.

She chucked her jacket and pack on the bed, put a Rory Todd cassette on her player, and got out her school folders. She wasn't normally so keen to do her homework, but maybe it would help take her mind off things.

Jas sat down and tried to concentrate on her work, but it was no good. She was too keyed up. What she needed was some gum to chew. She picked her jacket up from the bed and felt in her pocket for the packet. It wasn't there – but she did find the long, tubular shape of Gina's cigarette.

She took it out and looked at it. It was much longer than those she'd had before, and had a smart gold filter and logo. Gina had been right about it being a bit special.

Jas hesitated. In the last week or two she'd got quite used to smoking. It wasn't exactly the smoking itself she enjoyed – that still made her throat ache and her nose run. And she always felt guilty and furtive whenever she had a cigarette. But what Isabel had said was true. Smoking did make her feel more relaxed.

She looked at the cigarette Gina had given her again. She knew she shouldn't even be thinking about smoking at home. There'd be hell to pay if she got caught. But then again, there was no one around to catch her.

She ran downstairs and got the pack of matches that were kept in the drawer of the sideboard in the dining-room, for lighting candles at the dinner table on special occasions. She grabbed a saucer, too, and sped back up to her room again.

If she shut the door carefully and opened the window, no smoke would get into the rest of the house. And she could spray around with air freshener and brush her teeth when she'd finished. By the time the others came home, no one would be any the wiser.

Jas struck a match and lit up. As usual, the first couple of puffs made her cough, so she just sat there holding the cigarette and watching her reflection in the mirror. Why couldn't you just pose with a cigarette instead of having to smoke it? she wondered.

There was suddenly a sharp knock on her bedroom door, and before Jas even had time to jump, Abby put her head round. 'Have you seen the dictionary anywhere?' she asked.

Jas's hand, holding the cigarette, dropped down behind a pile of books stacked on the desk. Jas thought she was going to have a heart attack. Abby couldn't have spotted the cigarette – could she?

'I didn't think anyone else was home!' she squeaked. She could feel the hammer-like thump of the blood pounding through her veins.

'What?' Abby had the kind of distant, almost sleepy look she got when she'd been studying. 'I've had the afternoon off for revision.' Like a sleeper waking up, she took off her reading glasses and rubbed her eyes. Then she sniffed. 'Jas, are you smoking?'

'Me?' Jas held up her free hand innocently while she tried to stub the cigarette out behind the books with the other.

'Who else is in here?' Abby asked sarcastically, pushing her glasses up on to the top of her head. 'Or do you have a smoking ghost in this room?'

'Ha-ha,' Jas said, straight-faced. 'All that studying must have affected your sense of smell. You're always imagining you can smell smoke these days.'

'I'm not imagining it!' Abby pointed to the mirror on the wall behind Jas's desk.

Jas looked – and gulped. Reflected in the mirror was a clear view of her hand, clutching the cigarette.

'Are you going to tell me that studying has affected my eyesight?' Abby asked in a hollow tone.

Jas pushed the books away. She was surprised to feel tears rolling down her cheeks. Something inside her seemed to have snapped. All the anger and defiance that had kept her going for the last two weeks just seemed to run out, like a car running out of petrol, and all she was left with was unhappiness. 'Nothing else can go wrong now,' she managed to sob. 'You can tell Mum – I don't care what happens.'

Instead of being furious, as Jas had expected, Abby quietly stubbed the cigarette out and sat down on the bed. She patted the space beside her. 'What's going on, Jas? It's not like you to do this kind of thing. Want to tell me about it?'

Jas sat down beside her. She tried to wipe the tears away, but they wouldn't stop coming. After what seemed like ages, she finally managed to say, 'It's Gina . . .' and she began her long explanation.

'It sounds like a complete disaster,' Abby said, when she'd heard all about the competition, and Jas's feud with Liz and Becky and Charlie, and the way Gina had hijacked Jas's outfit, and all the other stories that came pouring out. She put her arm round Jas and gave her a hug. 'Even so, that doesn't change the fact that you've been smoking – and smoking's much more serious than the fashion competition. Smoking could kill you, but losing the fashion competition won't.'

'I know.' Jas's eyes were red and blotchy from

crying and her voice sounded even huskier than usual. 'I don't *really* want to smoke, it's just that all the others do it.'

'You mean Gina and Vale and Isabel do it,' Abby corrected her. Jas nodded. 'And do you want to be like them?'

Jas shook her head. 'No way. Gina's horrible.'

'Then why not stop?' Abby's dark brown eyes stared into Jas's bloodshot ones. 'I know that nothing I can say will make you stop if you don't want to – but I can't really believe you like it.'

'You're right, I don't.' Jas managed a smile. 'I'll give it up, Abby, I promise.' It was a surprise to experience a sudden surge of relief. Jas felt as if a weight had been lifted off her shoulders.

Abby gave her another hug. 'I'm pleased to hear it. But Gina and Vale won't be pleased. Are you sure you can cope with them getting at you if you don't want to take their cigarettes?'

'I don't care what they say any more,' Jas vowed firmly. 'You're not going to tell Mum and Dad about catching me smoking?' Jas asked.

'What's the point if you've given up?' Abby grinned. 'So long as you truly *have* given up, of course. If I catch you again, there'll be double hell to pay.'

'I know.' Jas managed a proper smile.

Abby was looking serious. 'What are you going to do about the fashion contest?'

Jas shrugged. 'If I want to be in it, I have to stay in Gina's team. So I'll just hope for the best.' She sighed and hiccuped. 'Thanks, Abby, for understanding.'

As she got up, Abby patted Jas on the head. 'That's what big sisters are for, isn't it?'

9

Jas peered into the mirror in the girls' cloakroom and applied just a touch more eyeliner. 'Watch it!' she exclaimed as Mina squeezed in beside her and jogged her elbow. 'Now I've got to start all over again,' she complained, mopping up the black smudge on her cheek.

'Sorry,' muttered Mina. 'It's too crowded in here.'

Jas tried again, using the eyeliner pencil Abby had lent her. In fact Abby had offered her all her make-up, and some jewellery to liven up the multi-coloured halter-neck top, too.

'Hey, Jas,' said Mina, as she turned round to go back to the changing room. 'Is that your sister's boyfriend out there, setting up the lights?'

Jas flinched a bit. 'Yes,' she admitted, anticipating laughter. Why had Stuart decided to wear his pink shorts today? She'd spotted them when she went past the hall earlier this afternoon and almost died of embarrassment.

'He's okay, isn't he?' Mina said, fixing up her long black hair. 'I thought he looked a bit of a wally at first, but then he explained all about the lights and taking photos and he was really nice. I wouldn't mind a boyfriend like him. If he finishes with your sister, let me know!'

'You're on,' Jas said, giggling.

'Yeah, I saw him too,' added Mina's friend Pritti. 'They've done a really good job, he and your sister.'

'Thanks,' Jas said, scooting away, surprised. What was it that everyone else saw in Stuart that she didn't? 'I'm all finished,' she announced to Isabel, when she returned to the girls' changing room. 'What do you think?'

'Awesome!' Isabel laughed. 'Jas, that eyeliner makes you look about eighteen!'

Most people were still waiting for their outfits to be brought down by Mrs Foster and Miss Hayden. Miss Tyler had decided it was easier if they brought everything down to the changing room, rather than having dozens of kids crowding the CDT classroom, searching for their outfits.

'I wonder how long we'll have to wait?' Isabel asked.

Gina glanced at Vale – and laughed when she caught her eye. There was something going on between the two of them, Jas felt sure. They were planning something – and it didn't take long to find out what.

Gina flung back her powder puff of hair. 'I don't have to wait at all,' she announced. 'Because I've got my outfit right here.' She opened the shopping bag she'd been carrying all day and pulled out a gorgeous off-the-shoulder Spanish-style dress made of shining gold fabric and decorated with edgings of beautiful black lace. It wasn't the kind of thing Jas would have worn, but she couldn't deny the fact that it was the loveliest thing she'd ever seen – more like a dream than a real dress.

119

'But you can't wear that!' she said, shaking her head in puzzled surprise.

'Oh, yes I can,' Gina responded, staring Jas straight in the eye as if defying her to disagree. 'I've had a last-minute change of plan and decided on a new outfit, that's all. There's nothing in the rules to say I can't do that.'

'But . . .' Jas stared at the beautiful lace and layers of fabric. 'You can't have made this in the last couple of days.'

'I did exactly what Emma did,' Gina said defiantly. 'I found a dress and adapted it to fit the theme.' Then Gina's face softened. 'Anyway, Jas, this new arrangement will suit you because now I'm wearing this, Vale's decided that she'll wear the Caribbean outfit instead. So you can have your silk top back again.'

'Really?' Jas couldn't quite believe it. She was delighted to think she was going to get the chance to wear her own design, but something still bothered her. There was no way she could believe that Gina had made the Spanish-style dress herself.

All the same, it was wonderful. On stage, under the lights, it would look amazing. And there was no doubt that it would make a big difference to their chances of winning the prize. Maybe on this occasion it was best to keep her suspicions to herself.

Her thoughts were interrupted by Miss Tyler, who came into the changing room looking serious. She hurried over to Liz Newman and her team and talked quietly with them for a moment. Then all five went out.

Jas wondered what was going on. The Mermaids

had looked upset. There was silence in the changing room as they walked out – and then the buzz began.

'What's happened?' Isabel asked. 'From Miss Tyler's face, you'd think someone had died.'

'I don't know.' Jas frowned. In the corner of the room she could see Gina and Vale sitting on the bench. They were the only two people in the whole place who didn't seem to be interested in what was going on.

A few seconds later Miss Tyler returned with her arm around a tearful Becky. Charlie, Liz and Emma followed, carrying their outfits. They all looked upset and angry.

And Jas gasped when she saw why. The outfits they were carrying were splattered with red paint. The changing room fell silent, except for surprised whispers.

'There's been a most unfortunate accident,' Miss Tyler announced. She, too, looked shaken. 'A pot of paint on a shelf above the area where I stored the costumes appears to have tipped over and damaged the Mermaids' outfits.'

'It doesn't look like an accident to me,' Charlie muttered, looking pale and tight-lipped. She glanced over at Gina and then at Jas.

Jas's eyebrows shot up. Charlie surely didn't think *she* had had anything to do with it?

Miss Tyler put her hand to her forehead. 'I agree that it looks very suspicious, but I don't know how it could have been deliberate. No one knew where the outfits were stored.'

Jas's heart jumped into her throat. Oh, yes they

did! She whipped round to confront Gina – and met an icy stare that silenced her.

'I hope *our* outfits are all right?' asked Vale, distracting attention.

Miss Tyler nodded. 'Yes, apart from a couple of tiny splashes, the other outfits seem to be fine – thank goodness.'

'What are we going to do?' Liz wailed, holding out her tablecloth skirt. It was covered in sticky paint. Emma's bathing costume was totally ruined, too.

'I'm afraid it's too late for us to change our plans. The fashion show has to go on.' Miss Tyler looked at the Mermaids sympathetically. 'I'm sorry, but . . .'

Becky burst into sobs and Liz looked as if she might crumble too. And Jas, watching them, felt as if she could explode with fury – because she had a strong suspicion who'd been responsible.

Just then Miss Hayden walked in, her arms full of clothing, and everyone gathered round to find their gear. In the fuss, Jas strode over to Gina and Vale. 'You did it, didn't you?' she demanded. 'You ruined their outfits.'

They both looked at her, wide-eyed with surprise – but to Jas it didn't seem convincing. 'How could we?' Vale asked. 'We didn't know where the outfits were stored.'

'Yes, you did,' Jas insisted. 'I told you they were in the CDT storeroom.'

'Did you?' Gina looked amazed. 'I don't remember . . .'

'Neither do I,' murmured Vale. 'When?'

'When we were on our way out of school on

Wednesday afternoon,' Jas snapped, getting increasingly furious with them for playing such silly games.

They both shook their heads. 'I don't remember it,' said Gina. 'Are you sure you're not imagining things?'

Jas could feel her fingers tightening into fists. Right now she just wanted to thump Gina straight on the nose.

Gina's puzzled expression cleared, as if a light had come on inside her head. 'If you knew where the outfits were being stored, *you* must have done it, Jas!' And she took a step backwards, looking appalled. 'How could you do something like that? It's terrible! And to think Liz and the others were your friends. I didn't know you had such a mean streak.'

The air seemed to get stuck in Jas's lungs, so that for a second she couldn't breathe. 'I didn't do it,' she grated, '*you* did.' Vale just smiled back innocently. Jas felt trapped. How could she prove anything without evidence? If the pair of them swore she was mistaken, there was nothing she could do about it.

Gina's eyes gleamed with cunning. 'Charlie's been having lots of trouble with Marco Guillano recently. Maybe *he* was the one who damaged their outfits. You know how nasty he can be when he's got it in for someone.'

Jas was momentarily sidetracked. It was true, from what she'd heard, that Marco was picking on Charlie.

'Well, personally, I think it was Miss Tyler's fault,' said Vale, sighing. 'I mean, fancy putting beautiful clothes like that in the same place she stores

123

paint and glue and all sorts of messy things. There was bound to be an accident.'

'Who knows what happened?' Gina shrugged.

Jas watched, feeling shaken and angry and helpless. There seemed to be nothing she could say or do that wouldn't get *her* into trouble. She looked around. Most people were already dressed in their outfits, ready for the fashion show.

'Don't worry about a thing.' Gina's thin white fingers bit into Jas's arm. 'Let's just get dressed up and concentrate on winning the first prize.'

'Next team,' whispered Miss Hayden, beckoning Jas, Gina, Vale and Isabel forward. They were standing in the wings of the school stage, waiting their turn to go in the fashion show.

Jas glanced round the edge of the flats at the side of the stage. The hall was dark, but the catwalk was brightly lit by Stuart's lamps. Every few seconds, she saw the flash of his camera as he took photos of Ryan's team, lumbering around in their moon outfits in time to the music.

They were having a few problems. A length of stretchy vacuum cleaner hose had dropped off Jamie Thompson's outfit and tripped him up, and Ryan's space helmet, which he'd made from a cardboard box, had tipped over his eyes. As his hands were encased in huge silvery cardboard gloves he was having difficulty straightening it. Clinton had to grab him to stop him falling off the edge of the stage.

Everyone was roaring with laughter as Miss Tyler described their outfits and there was a huge round of applause as they came clumping back up the opposite side of the stage. 'Get me out of here!' Ryan was protesting in a muffled voice as they fell backstage. Jas had to stifle a giggle, because it was her turn next.

'Go!' instructed Miss Hayden, and Gina flounced her way into the spotlights, followed by Vale in the halter-necked outfit, Isabel in her Sixties dress and, bringing up the rear, Jas in the sand-coloured silk top and cycle shorts, with Gina's shell necklace.

'Here come the Millionaires!' announced Miss Tyler, who was really getting into the swing of things as the show's MC. 'First we have Gina Galloway from 2K. Gina's wearing a sand-coloured flared top, hand-painted with starfish and shells—' Miss Tyler did a double-take. 'Oh, no, she's not!' There was a roar of laughter from the audience. 'Umm, Gina's wearing a gold flamenco-style dress, perfect for a holiday in Spain . . .'

There were oohs and aahs as Gina swayed down the stage in her dress. Under the spotlights it looked more gorgeous than ever. So did all the sparkling jewellery Gina had borrowed from her mother.

Jas, too, got a big round of applause from the audience as she danced down the catwalk. No matter what had been going on, she was determined to have a good time. With a big grin she twirled round so that the top flew out in a bell shape. Stuart's camera flashed a dozen times as she danced towards him, and as she got to the end she heard Abby's voice crying, 'Yeah, way to go, Jas!'

Backstage, all the competitors were crowding round

125

waiting to hear the results. It was taking ages for the three judges to make up their minds.

'What's the problem?' Gina yawned. 'It's obvious we're the best team.'

Jas's stomach was a tight knot of tension. She desperately wanted to win the contest, of course. Ever since the day it had been announced, that had been her aim. But her suspicions about Gina made her worry, too.

As she was standing there wishing she had some gum to chew, the judges seemed to reach a decision. Mr Leach climbed the four steps to the stage and held out a sheet of paper.

'We've all seen some spectacular outfits this afternoon,' he announced. 'Miss Tyler, Miss Diamond and I would like to say how much we enjoyed all of them. We particularly liked the imagination of Ryan Bryson's team, who dressed for a holiday on the Moon, and the team from 1D who dressed as famous monuments – we thought the Eiffel Tower costume was particularly clever.'

'We also wish we'd had the opportunity to see the outfits made by the Mermaids team from 2K, which were accidentally ruined. Perhaps the Mermaids would like to stand up and take a bow anyway.' Peering from behind the stage, Jas watched as Liz, Becky, Charlie and Emma, all of them white-faced, stood up in their places in the front row. There was a sympathetic round of applause for them.

As they sat down again, Mr Leach continued. 'And now for the overall winners – the team who will represent Bell Street School in the regional

126

heats of the *Threads* Young Designer of the Year competition . . .'

Jas held her breath and the knot inside her stomach tightened so much that it hurt.

'The winning team is – the Millionaires!' Jas wasn't sure she'd heard right, until Gina grabbed her hand.

'Come on,' she instructed. 'Didn't I tell you there was no way we weren't going to win?'

'Hold this,' instructed Gina, stepping out of her gold dress. She shoved it at Jas, who'd already slipped out of the silk top.

Jas took the dress from Gina and admired it again. It was lovely. And beautifully made. Inside, the seams were finished off neatly, and it was even lined. Not like her own top, which definitely had a home-made look if you saw it turned inside out.

All Jas's suspicions came flooding back. Gina had admitted that the dress was bought. But she'd said she changed it. What had she done? Jas gave it a quick inspection. From what she could see, there was no sign of any alterations. Just a few green threads at the back of the neck, as if someone had snipped a label away.

'What are you looking at, nosey?' Gina demanded, seizing the dress from her and stuffing it into the bag.

Jas bit her lip. 'Do you seriously think you can get away with it?' she asked quietly.

'With what?' Two tell-tale red spots had appeared on Gina's cheeks.

'With buying a dress and pretending that you've made it yourself,' Jas spelled out.

'I told you, I made some alterations,' Gina hissed. 'And if you don't say anything, no one's going to know, are they?'

Jas's eyebrows shot halfway up her forehead. 'But, Gina, you can't do things like that!' she argued, trying to keep her voice down so they wouldn't be overheard.

'Quit moaning,' Gina growled. 'Look, Jas, I don't see what you're worried about. I won the competition for us, didn't I? And that's all that matters.'

'No it's not.' Jas shook her head. 'It's cheating.'

Gina shrugged. 'So what? I bet half the outfits in this contest were made by people's mums, anyway. I don't see there's any real difference.'

Jas opened her mouth to register another protest, but Gina put her finger firmly over her lips. She pushed her face so close to Jas's, Jas could feel the tickly brush of pale, fluffy hair on her forehead.

'Not another word – otherwise I'm going to send my mum straight round to your house to discuss your smoking problem with your mum.' Gina imitated her own mother's voice. ' "*I thought you ought to know, Mrs Scott, that I found Jasmine smoking in my house . . .*" How would you like that?' she asked. There was a flicker of triumph in Gina's eyes. She knew perfectly well that there was no way Jas could risk that happening.

'Jas?' Abby knocked on the door of Jas's bedroom.

'What do you want?' Jas was lying on the bed, listening to a cassette and hoping all her problems would go away – because there was nothing she could do to sort them out.

128

'Can we come in?' It was Stuart's voice. He stuck his head round the door. 'Why are you looking so miserable?' he asked, sounding serious. 'We thought you'd be out celebrating!'

'I've got no one to celebrate with – and I don't want to talk to Gina ever again.' Jas sat up as they came in.

'Actually, it was Gina we wanted to talk to you about.' Abby leaned against Jas's desk. She was holding a rolled-up magazine.

'I don't even want to hear anything about that girl,' Jas groaned, picking up the pillow and putting it over her head.

'Okay,' Stuart said with a laugh. 'Shall we tell you how great you looked, instead?'

'Yes,' Abby agreed, 'your outfit was brilliant. But I thought you'd said Gina had decided *she* was going to wear your sandy-coloured top. I nearly fell over backwards when I saw that dress she had on. It was pretty amazing.'

Jas shook her head. 'It's a long story,' she said, sighing. 'She just suddenly said she'd changed her mind and made a new outfit. It's the kind of thing she does. I don't understand what's really going on.'

Pursing her lips, Abby said, 'Well, I think I do.' She held out the magazine she'd been holding – one of the expensive American ones Jas saved up for. She'd bought it earlier in the week, but hadn't yet read it. 'Have a look at this.'

Jas looked – and looked again. Under the headline 'Kiff Rowan's Collection for a New Europe' there were several pictures of willowy models prancing up and down the catwalk. As usual, Kiff Rowan's new

129

designs were gorgeous. One picture in particular stood out from all the others. It showed a gold Spanish-style dress, with touches of black lace.

'Uh-oh.' Jas stared up at Abby. 'I can't believe Gina's so stupid! Does she really think that no one's going to notice that she's wearing a designer outfit?'

'I don't know.' Abby held out her hands in a gesture of disbelief. 'But the moment I saw that dress, I knew she hadn't made it. It was too good to be true. On the way home, I began to remember seeing this picture in your magazine. You left it downstairs on the coffee table and I was looking through it the other day.'

Stuart spoke. 'You're going to have to tell Miss Tyler, Jas. Sooner or later someone's going to find out. It's not only going to make Gina look stupid, but it'll damage the school's reputation. You don't want people saying that Bell Street kids are cheats, do you?'

'And if you don't say anything, they might think you helped plan it,' Abby added.

'I know, I know.' Jas bit her lip. They were right. For more reasons than they were aware of, Gina had to be stopped.

'You'll tell Miss Tyler on Monday?' Abby asked.

Jas looked up like a sad-eyed puppy. Her glance went from Abby to Stuart. But what did it matter now? 'I told Gina I didn't think she'd made that dress herself, and she told me that if I said a word, she'll tell Mum I was smoking.'

Stuart didn't look surprised. 'Abby told me she'd caught you in the act,' he said. He didn't sound very bothered.

130

Jas frowned. 'Don't we have any secrets around here?' she demanded, glancing at Abby.

'Don't worry,' Abby said calmly, 'Stuart's not going to tell anyone else. I just wanted his advice about what to do.'

'And I told her not to get too wound up about it,' Stuart said mildly, flopping down on the bed. 'A couple of cigarettes doesn't exactly make you a hardened smoker.'

'I've stopped, anyway,' Jas informed him firmly. 'But Mum won't listen to that. You know what she's like. If she hears a word about me touching a cigarette, she'll go through the roof.'

Abby, though, had made up her mind. 'It's going to cause extra trouble, but you're going to have to do it,' she said gently. 'Miss Tyler's got to know that Gina's been cheating. There's no way out.'

But Stuart put his hand to his head. 'Hold on,' he said, a broad grin crossing his face. 'I've had an idea.'

'What is it?' Jas wanted to know.

He looked mysterious. 'I'm not going to tell you,' he said. 'Just wait and see.'

10

'The next round of the fashion competition's going to be held in Birmingham,' Gina was telling Emma in a loud voice as Jas walked into class on Monday morning. 'My mum knows a very good hotel there, with a swimming-pool and sauna and a restaurant that does the best food ever, so we'll probably stay overnight there. I don't know what the other people in the team will do,' she finished with a condescending smile as Jas went past. 'Morning, Jas. That's a lovely jacket you're wearing.'

'Morning, Gina.' Jas managed a grim smile. The Kiff Rowan jacket had cheered her up a little bit – but not enough to make her happy to see Gina.

'I was just telling Emma about the next round in the *Threads* contest.' Gina stood over Jas as she slid into her seat. 'It sounds like fun. They look at each team and choose the best outfit of the four. Then the team representatives appear in a fashion show, and they choose the best five to go to London for the TV final.'

'And what do you plan to wear for the next round?' Jas asked acidly.

For a second Gina looked confused. 'What do you mean?' she asked.

Jas shrugged and looked as innocent as she could.

'Well, you just seem to have trouble making up your mind what to wear.'

'Very funny,' Gina growled. 'Maybe I'll wear your silk top.' It was meant as another threat, Jas knew – and she was sick of it.

The first lesson of the day was Design, with Miss Tyler. 'Who remembered to bring in some packaging from home?' she asked, scanning the class. A few hands, clutching boxes and wrappers and plastic pots, shot up. 'Good,' she said, nodding. 'Let's start with washing-powder packs. If you've got one of those with you, stand up and hold them out so that everyone can see them.'

Jas got to her feet. She'd remembered to grab the almost-empty box of Dazzle powder as she'd left the house.

'Take a close look at them,' Miss Tyler instructed.

The lesson was interrupted by a brisk knock at the door. It was Mr Heyward, the history teacher, looking rather cross. But then he always looked cross. That was why the kids at Bell Street called him 'Happy' Heyward.

'This was just delivered to the staff room for you,' he grumbled, handing Miss Tyler a brown envelope. 'Apparently it's very urgent.'

Looking surprised, Miss Tyler took the envelope. 'Thank you, Mr Heyward.' She turned back to the class. 'While I see what this is, I'd like you to make a list of the design features the washing-powder packets share.'

Jas picked up her pencil, but she didn't start writing. She was curious to know what so urgently required Miss Tyler's attention – and so was the rest of the class, judging by the nudges and giggles as they watched their teacher pull the envelope open.

She pulled a magazine out of the packet – a magazine that made Jas sit bolt upright in surprise. On the front of it, there was a note, attached with a paper clip. Jas sat there, open-mouthed, her mind racing. This had to be something to do with Stuart!

Miss Tyler adjusted her red-rimmed glasses, read the note and then opened the magazine and looked at something. Jas knew exactly what. She cast a quick glance back at Gina, whose face was as pale and composed as a mask. Maybe she didn't know that the picture was in the magazine, but Jas doubted it.

Then Miss Tyler read the note again. Finally, she said in a firm voice, 'Put your pencils down, everyone, please.'

There was an ominous silence. Everyone, even Ryan and Clinton, who normally lounged across their desks, sat up and folded their arms.

'Gina Galloway, would you come here, please?' Miss Tyler sounded very calm.

Gina came slowly down the aisle, holding her chin up high. She had a fixed, but not very convincing, smile. 'Yes, Miss Tyler?'

'Would you look at this picture?' Miss Tyler held out the magazine. When Gina looked up, she had two bright red spots of colour in her cheeks.

'Does that dress look familiar to you?' Miss Tyler asked.

Gina looked as if she might explode. 'A bit,' she said.

Jas began to feel jubilant. There was no way Gina could get out of this. She'd been caught red-handed.

Miss Tyler raised her eyebrows. 'Only a bit? I'm not a great expert, but I'd say it was *exactly* like the dress you wore in the competition on Friday.' There was an instant buzz that echoed round the room, as if someone had just disturbed a beehive. 'Was yours a Kiff Rowan dress?' Miss Tyler asked directly.

'What if it was?' Gina replied. 'You said it was okay for Emma to buy an outfit and adapt it, so I just did the same.' There was uproar in the classroom. Liz and Becky and Charlie and Emma were looking outraged.

So was Miss Tyler. 'I take cheating very seriously,' she said, tight-lipped with anger. 'Did any of the others in your team know about this?'

'Jas did,' Gina replied instantly.

Jas opened her mouth wide in surprise. She should have suspected Gina would try to land her with the blame!

'Were you in on Gina's plan?' Miss Tyler asked her. For a moment, Jas panicked. Was she going to end up in terrible trouble, just as Gina had threatened all along?

'No!' she said quickly. Her shock was evident to everyone watching. 'I did suspect that Gina hadn't made the dress, but when I asked her about it she said she had.'

'I said I'd adapted it – just like Emma did,' Gina pouted. 'You said it was okay for her to do that, so I don't understand why I'm not allowed to do the same thing.'

Miss Tyler took another look at the picture in the

135

magazine. 'From this, I can't see what you adapted.'

'She cut out the label,' Jas said quickly. The kids in the class giggled. Gina's glare was intended to cut her in half, but it didn't work.

'Why didn't you come and tell me this as soon as you had your suspicions?' Miss Tyler wanted to know.

Jas was silent for a moment. It was no good saying that Gina had threatened to tell about her smoking – that would just make things ten times as bad. 'I couldn't prove anything,' she said. 'I told Gina she should own up, but . . .'

'You're a sneak,' growled Gina. Miss Tyler held out a silencing finger.

'Do you know anything about the 'accident' that happened to Liz's team's outfits, Jas?' Miss Tyler asked. Jas could feel the Mermaids' eyes boring into her.

'No,' she said honestly. 'I didn't touch them, Miss Tyler. I don't know for certain who did, but . . .' She looked straight at Gina before turning to Liz and Becky. 'I'm really sorry about what happened to your things. You should have won the competition.'

Liz smiled resignedly. Charlie and Becky just stared. They made Jas feel like a traitor.

Gina rolled her eyes. 'I never wanted you in my team in the first place,' she muttered. 'You're a total creep, Jas.'

'That's irrelevant,' Miss Tyler inserted sharply. 'Jasmine, I don't think you have anything to be proud of. You should have acted immediately on your suspicions, not waited for someone from outside the school to draw my attention to what's been going

136

on. I'm surprised and very disappointed by your behaviour. You're the kind of student I thought I could trust to know the difference between right and wrong.'

Jas hung her head. Miss Tyler was right. She should have known better. And yet after all she'd been through, with Gina bossing her about and theatening her, to get such a public ticking-off didn't seem fair. Her ears were hot with embarrassment and tears stung her eyes.

'And as for you, Gina, I think this is a matter Mr Leach needs to know about. As soon as this lesson has ended, you'll come with me to see him. I think you can both take it that your team will be disqualified from the fashion competition.' Miss Tyler was looking more stern than Jas could ever remember her.

Gina's eyes blazed with silvery defiance. As she came back up the aisle past Jas's desk, she aimed a sharp kick – but Jas pulled her foot away, and Gina just bruised her toes on the metal leg. She breathed a sigh of relief.

Surely this was the end of the whole, horrible fashion show saga?

'You creep!' As Jas rounded the corner of the science block, Gina reached out and grabbed her by her backpack, bringing her to a halt. Gina was livid – Jas could almost see steam coming out of her ears.

Gina's sharp fingers shot out and pinched Jas's neck. 'Ow!' She jumped back. 'Just leave me alone!' Jas cried. 'I've had more than enough of you and your mean tricks.'

'I'm not going to leave you alone,' Gina hissed.

'I'm on report till the end of term because of you
– and so is Vale. And Mr Leach called our parents
and asked them to come and see him later in the
week. All because you sneaked about my dress.'

'It wasn't me,' Jas protested, keeping her distance.
'I didn't send that magazine. I was sitting in class
with you when it was delivered.'

'Then who did?'

'Someone who knows something about fashion, I
suppose.' Jas put her hands on her hips and chewed
angrily on her gum. 'Anyway, I'm glad the Millionaires are out of the competition. I hate cheats just
as much as Miss Tyler.'

Gina was so furious that Jas could see the pulse in
her neck. 'Don't think you've got away with it,' she
spat. 'I said I'd tell your mum that you smoke, and
I will.'

'My mum wouldn't believe a word from a liar like
you.' Jas didn't bat an eyelid. 'I'll just tell her that
you've got it in for me.' She suddenly felt quite brave.
After all, what did she have to fear from Gina now?
No one would take her seriously now she'd been
shown up.

Gina looked her up and down. Then those silvery
eyes narrowed calculatingly. 'All right,' she nodded.
'In that case I'll tell my mum that you stole my very
expensive Kiff Rowan jacket while you were working
round at our house.' Her eyes were focused on the
jacket's discreet embroidered logo.

Jas winced. She loved the jacket. She'd worn it
several times since Gina had lent it to her, and
it always made her feel confident and good about
herself. It hurt to take it off and give it back to

Gina – but she had to do it. There was no other way.

'Here, have it,' she said flatly, before walking away so that Gina didn't see the tears in her eyes.

It was the jacket that had got her into all this. If she hadn't been so easily blinded by fancy labels, she would have been able to see that Gina was just using her. What a fool she'd been to imagine that anything good would ever come from it . . .

'Well, what happened?' Abby and Stuart came in from college and stood in front of the TV, their arms round each others' waists. They looked very, *very* pleased with themselves.

'It *was* you, wasn't it?' Jas exclaimed. 'You were the ones who sent Miss Tyler the magazine.'

'*Us?*' Stuart tried to look innocent. 'I don't know what you're talking about.' But his big grin betrayed him.

'I thought it had to be your plan,' Jas said with a laugh. 'The moment I saw the magazine. It couldn't have been anyone else.'

Abby was looking frustrated. 'You still haven't told us what happened. Did Gina get caught?'

'Yeah, what did Miss Tyler say?' asked Stuart. 'I'd love to have been there to see how she reacted.' Stuart sat down in a leather armchair and pulled Abby into his lap.

'Miss Tyler went mad and accused Gina of cheating, and then Gina said *I'd* known all about it . . .' Jas ran through the whole scene. Abby and Stuart listened to it with obvious pleasure.

'It worked perfectly, then,' Abby said when Jas had finished. 'Gina's off your back and out of the contest. And all because of Stuart's bright idea.' She patted his cheek affectionately.

'I'm glad that bad-tempered teacher actually delivered the magazine.' Stuart beamed. 'I took it up to the school on my motorbike and hammered on the staff-room door. When he came out and I asked if it would be possible to get the envelope to Miss Tyler urgently, he looked as if he'd like to murder me.'

'He might have done, too,' Jas said, giggling. 'There's a rumour that some kids have gone into Mr Heyward's history class, never to come out again.'

Stuart whistled. 'Sounds as if I was lucky to escape, then!'

'What did your note say?' Jas asked.

'Just that I'd seen a picture of Gina's dress in the magazine and I thought Miss Tyler might be interested. I signed it myself. There's no reason why she should think you had anything to do with it.'

'Well,' said Abby, rubbing her hands, 'that's that. Maybe now Gina will leave you alone and stop all these stupid threats.'

Jas looked uncertain. 'I don't trust her one inch. She always likes to have the final say in everything.'

'You sound as if you're getting paranoid,' Abby said with a laugh. 'Gina's only human! Even she's got to admit defeat at some point.'

But Jas still wasn't convinced. Gina wouldn't take this lying down, she felt sure.

'Well,' Stuart said, reaching for his bag, 'I'll tell you what'll make her really mad. I printed up some of the shots I took on Friday.'

'Can I have a look at them?' Jas was itching to see what they looked like.

'Sure.' Stuart spread them out on the table.

'Why do you think Gina's going to go mad about these?' Jas wanted to know.

Stuart picked one up. 'The local paper thought this was the best. It'll be on their front page on Friday.'

'Who is it?' Jas turned his hand over to see. 'Wow! It's me!'

11

Wetherton market was always busy, whatever the time of day. Jas wandered among the stalls after school on Thursday, but somehow they didn't seem as interesting as usual. She felt lonely, walking round on her own. Even her favourite stall, the one that sold leggings and cropped tops and fun jewellery, didn't seem worth stopping at today.

I might as well go home, Jas decided, mooching past the smelly fish stand. She slid between a fruit stall and one selling household goods and gadgets and came out opposite the Indian stall. That, anyway, was what she and the gang used to call it, because it sold long flowery skirts and scarves and incense from India. Charlie often bought things there.

Jas walked over to inspect the shirts and jackets hanging on the rail. There was a boxy black jacket that caught her eye. It wasn't exactly up to Kiff Rowan's standard of design, but it was worth looking at more closely.

Jas pulled the hanger – and someone on the other side of the rail pulled it back again. 'It's stuck,' said a voice, and several voices burst out laughing.

Jas recognised them immediately. She pulled back some of the garments on the rail and peered through to the other side.

For a moment the laughter froze as her eyes met those of Becky, Liz and Charlie. All four of them stood there uncomfortably. Jas swallowed hard. It felt as if she had a lump in her throat, threatening to choke her.

'Hi,' she managed to say. It made her feel sad and left out just to see them together like that. After all, they always used to come to the market together. She really missed them.

And maybe that was what they needed to know. 'I've really been missing you,' she murmured, feeling her eyes glaze over. Unless she was careful, she'd cry. 'I don't suppose there's any chance of you forgiving me?'

Liz's eyes twinkled. 'Well, we've been watching you watching us across the playground.'

Becky was looking less hostile, too. 'Yeah, we've been wondering how long it would take before you cracked and said sorry.'

'She hasn't said sorry yet!' Charlie pointed out.

Jas raced round the rail of clothes. 'Of course I'm sorry for what happened,' she said softly. 'I got so carried away with wanting to win the competition. And after I'd joined up with Gina she was just awful to me. I've never been so miserable in my life. I wish I'd stuck with you.' She could hear herself rabbiting on. 'And your outfits were great, you know. You should have won the contest.'

'We know that.' Charlie said indignantly. 'We were so mad at you for switching teams and joining Gina that we decided we were going to beat you.'

'And we would have done, if you hadn't sabotaged

our outfits.' A touch of ice returned to Liz's voice.

'I didn't have anything to do with it,' Jas vowed. 'But I'm pretty sure Gina and Vale did.'

'That's what we figured.' Becky put her hands in her pockets. 'What made you want to hang out with them in the first place, Jas? You knew what they were like.'

'They were really enthusiastic about my ideas – more than the three of you.' Jas said, wincing. 'To begin with, at least. Then Gina began to get nasty.'

'Surprise, surprise!' Becky almost giggled.

'A great friend you turned out to be,' Liz summed up in a grumpy voice. But she looked more friendly than she sounded.

'Well, if *you're* such great friends, why didn't you come and rescue me when you could see how miserable I was?' Jas demanded, aware of how silly the conversation was becoming.

Becky laughed. 'We wanted to make sure you learned your lesson properly.'

'I promise you I have!' Jas grinned ruefully and shifted her weight from one foot to the other. 'Look, can we be friends again?'

'Oooh, I don't know,' teased Charlie, tilting her head on one side. 'I mean, you've really changed, Jas. You're not the person we used to know. All this showing off with Gina Galloway and smoking—'

'I've given it all up,' Jas cut in. 'I promise you, I'll never touch another cigarette – and I'm certainly never going near Gina Galloway again!'

The others looked at each other. 'What do you think?' asked Liz, sounding dubious. But there was something about their manner that made Jas certain they were just fooling around with her.

'I think we'll give you a second chance,' Charlie said, trying to sound grudging.

'Me too!' Becky giggled, and stepped over to hug her.

'Yeah – after all, we reckon you had something to do with the magazine that was delivered to Miss Tyler,' Liz laughed.

Jas was surprised. 'How did you know?' she asked. 'It was supposed to be a secret.'

Charlie shrugged. 'You and Gina are the only people we know who read fancy fashion magazines like that. It had to be Gina or you – and you don't need to be a genius to know it wasn't Gina.'

'Actually it was Stuart who delivered the magazine,' Jas explained. 'He and Abby were the first to spot the photo and match it up with Gina's dress.'

'Stuart?' Charlie's face lit up. 'What a clever guy he is.'

'He's okay,' Jas agreed. She supposed Stuart wasn't so bad after all.

'He was really nice to us,' Becky chipped in. 'When he heard what had happened to our outfits, he said he'd try and think of some way of making it up to us.'

'Abby's really lucky to have met someone like him,' said Charlie, wistfully. 'Aren't you pleased she's got someone like him around?'

Jas frowned. She'd never really thought of it that way. But yes, she was. It was good to know Abby had found someone who made her so obviously happy. Even if that did leave Jas feeling pretty excluded.

'In a way,' Liz changed the subject, 'I was quite relieved that we didn't have to take part in the fashion show. I was really nervous about everyone staring at me. That bra made out of paper plates was quite daring.'

Becky and Charlie looked at her in disbelief. 'You didn't tell *us* you felt that way,' said Becky.

Jas put her arms round her friends – her real friends. 'What a terrible mess it's all turned out to be,' she said with a sigh.

They nodded in agreement. 'Even though we were so mad at you, we still missed you.' Liz squeezed her hand. 'The Mermaids weren't the same without you.'

Jas thought she was going to start crying from sheer relief. It was so good to be back with her friends. 'One thing's for sure,' she said, dabbing her eyes, 'I'm never going to let anything like this happen again.'

'Just try it,' Charlie said with a laugh.

'Can I go swimming with Liz and Becky?' Jas called from the hall. She was on the phone and her mother was in the kitchen, doing the Saturday morning chores. Abby was doing her set job of hoovering the sitting room – with a bit of help from Stuart. Everyone had to shout over the noise of the Hoover.

'How are you going to get there?' Mrs Scott shouted back.

'Becky's dad's taking us.'

'Okay,' agreed Mrs Scott. 'Where's your games kit, Jas? I'm just loading the washing machine.'

'In my backpack, in the living room.' Jas turned back to the receiver. 'Yes, it's all right, I can come.'

'We'll pick you up at the end of your road in half an hour then,' Becky said.

Jas raced into the sitting room. Her mum was unzipping her pack. 'I need that to put my swimming gear in,' she explained, pulling her joggers and T-shirt out of the pack and handing them to her mum. A load of other things fell out on the floor. Pens, notebooks, cassettes, a cutting from a magazine, a headphone set from her personal stereo . . . Jas just grabbed everything and shoved it back in without really looking. It was only the usual stuff she carried around.

But Mrs Scott had spotted something. 'Hold on a second.' She pulled the pack away from Jas. 'Is that a cigarette lighter you've got there?'

Abby switched off the vacuum cleaner. 'That's this room done,' she said, rubbing her hands. 'Stuart and I are going out now, okay?'

But Mrs Scott wasn't listening. She'd plunged her hand into the pack and was ferreting around. 'Mum!' Jas protested. 'What are you doing?'

'I'm sure I saw a cigarette lighter. It was caught up in your stereo headphones.' Mrs Scott frowned at Jas. 'What are you doing carrying all this junk around with you every day, anyway?'

'It's not junk, it's useful,' Jas protested. 'And I haven't got a lighter in there.' She wasn't bothered. Her mother must have seen something else – an eraser or a packet of gum or something that looked like a lighter.

'Aaah!' Mrs Scott peered into the depths of the pack and withdrew her hand. 'What are these, then?'

She placed two items on the table: a long, thin

cigarette pack covered in shiny gold foil with a distinctive logo, and a cheap green plastic cigarette lighter. Jas just stared at them, astonished. Where had they come from?

Her mother stared squarely at her. 'I'd like an explanation, Jas,' she said with the kind of quiet tone that both Jas and Abby had learned to dread. 'And it had better be a good one.' When Mrs Scott used that very calm, measured voice, it usually meant that *someone* was in deep, deep trouble.

'They're not mine.' Jas began to panic inside. How could she convince her mother that they were nothing to do with her? Jas hadn't touched a cigarette since the day Abby had caught her smoking upstairs in her room.

She took a quick glance at Abby, who was looking almost as thunderous as her mother. Jas could guess exactly what Abby was thinking – that she'd lied and been smoking behind her back all the while.

'Honestly, Mum!' What else could she say? She rubbed her eyes, in case it was all a horrible dream, but the cigarettes were still there, lying accusingly on the table. Just then Stuart stepped forward.

'Oh, I wondered where those had got to,' he said, picking up the packet and the lighter.

'They're yours?' Mrs Scott looked amazed – but no more so than Jas and Abby.

'Yes.' Stuart looked surprised that they were so surprised. 'Don't you remember, Jas? I popped them into your bag when I was up at school last week setting up the lights for the fashion show. Old Wiggy Leach didn't want me smoking, so you put them out of the way for me.'

148

'Yeah?' asked Jas, unable to make sense of what was happening. She deliberately hadn't been into the school hall while Stuart and Abby were working there. Then, noticing the way he was nodding encouragingly at her, she said more firmly, 'Oh, yes, I'd forgotten all about it. I must have been carrying them round with me all that time.'

Mrs Scott stared at Stuart, perplexed. 'I didn't know you smoked,' she said accusingly.

Even Stuart gulped. Mrs Scott on the warpath was an awesome sight. 'Well,' he said slowly, 'I'm not a heavy smoker, but I do like one occasionally. And I know you and Mr Scott don't like smoking, so I never smoke while I'm here.'

'I see.' Mrs Scott fixed Abby with her dark eyes. 'Abby, you haven't started smoking too, have you?'

'No!' Abby exclaimed, insulted. 'I have not!' She glared at both Stuart and Jas. 'Stuart never smokes when he's with me,' she added pointedly.

'I must say that I'm very surprised. And disappointed, too, Stuart,' Mrs Scott said with a frown. But she seemed pleased that it was neither of her daughters who was at fault. 'I suppose you're old enough to make your own decisions,' she admitted. 'If you know the dangers of smoking and you're still foolish enough to take the risk, there's nothing I can do.'

'Mmm,' Stuart nodded, looking apologetic.

Mrs Scott gathered up Jas's gym kit. 'In future, please don't ask Jas to look after your cigarettes. Just think of the trouble she could have got into if someone at school had found them.'

'Yes,' said Stuart with the hint of a smile. 'Can you imagine what Miss Tyler would say?'

Jas raised her eyebrows. It was too horrible to think about.

'I'd better get on with the washing.' Mrs Scott went back to the kitchen.

Jas stared at the other two in complete confusion. 'What's going on?' she said.

'But you don't smoke, Stuart.' Abby was still puzzled as she, Stuart and Jas walked down to the end of the road together.

'I know!' Stuart grinned. 'But it seemed the easiest way to distract your mum from Jas. One look at your face, Jas, and I knew you were as surprised to see those cigarettes as your mum was.'

'I thought I was seeing things when she pulled them out,' Jas confessed.

Abby still looked puzzled. 'What were the cigarettes doing there in the first place? You haven't started smoking again, have you, Jas? After the promise you made?'

Jas shook her head. 'No, I haven't touched one since then. And as for how they got into my bag, I don't know. But I'm pretty sure I know who put them there.'

'Who?' Abby and Stuart both asked.

'Gina. Who else would have done it?' Jas's dark eyebrows were furrowed. 'She could have slipped them into my bag when I left it in the gym changing room, or when I was in the CDT workshop. I wouldn't put anything past her.'

Abby grimaced. 'There's nothing you can do. You can't be sure they were hers, after all.'

'Yes I can,' Jas nodded, feeling more and more

certain. 'Have a look at the packet. Gina told me it's the most expensive brand of cigarettes you can buy. Who else would have them but Gina?'

Stuart took the box out of his pocket. 'You're right, they look special,' he nodded, taking one of the three remaining cigarettes out of the pack. 'And look, they've got a flashy gold filter.'

'Gina's mum bought some in London and she stole a pack – at least, that's what she told me. I bet you can't buy them anywhere in Wetherton,' Jas said firmly.

Abby had been digesting all this. 'You mean Gina hid those cigarettes in your backpack hoping that you'd get caught?'

'Yeah. It sounds just the kind of thing Gina would do.' Jas laughed grimly. 'And it nearly worked. She didn't reckon on Stuart coming to the rescue like that, though. Thanks, Stuart.' She smiled at him warmly. 'You're a hero – just like Abby's always said.'

'That's okay.' He went a bit pink and squeezed Abby's hand. 'After you'd given Abby your word that you'd given up smoking, I felt sure that these didn't belong to you. But I could see your mum was going to give you a very hard time if you couldn't explain where they'd come from. So I just said the first thing that came into my head.'

'And got a telling-off for your trouble!' Abby giggled. She had that soft, gooey look that Jas used to think was ridiculous – but which she was now just beginning to understand. 'Oh, Stuart, you *are* stupid – and kind, and thoughtful and brave. Mum might have made mincemeat of you.' Abby put her arms round him and gave him a kiss.

Jas watched them and couldn't help feeling soppy too – and pleased for Abby that she'd found herself such a nice boyfriend. It was great to see Abby looking so happy.

'I'm really sorry for all the times I've been nasty to you,' Jas told Stuart when Abby had let him go. 'Like that chilli burger I gave you. I don't know what made me do it.'

He smiled down at her and ruffled her hair. It was strange – because looking at him now, Jas realised that he was actually quite handsome. Maybe he had sandy-coloured hair and thin legs, but there was something about him, something that everyone except her seemed to recognise almost as soon as they met him.

'It's only natural for you to resent me,' he said gently. 'After all, I'm taking so much of Abby's time and attention. You're not getting your fair share of it any more. So you see, I understood why you weren't particularly pleased with me.'

Jas opened her mouth but could think of nothing more to say. She was beginning to appreciate why Abby felt so good when Stuart was around.

They came to the end of the street. 'Do you want us to wait with you till Becky and her dad come?' Abby asked.

Jas shook her head. 'There's no need. They should be here at any moment.' Then a thought began to form in her mind. 'Would you let me have the cigarettes and lighter?'

'You're not going to start smoking again, are you?' Abby asked suspiciously. Then she realised how bossy she sounded. 'Sorry, Jas, but I worry about you – I don't want to see you start something that could ruin your life.'

Jas laughed. 'I promise you, I'm not going to smoke them.'

'You've got a plan, haven't you?' Stuart guessed.

Jas shrugged casually. 'It's nothing complicated. I thought I'd just give them back to Gina, that's all.'

Jas led the way up the Galloway's drive to the impressive front door.

'Well, her mum's car is here, anyway,' said Liz, pointing to the glossy white saloon parked by the garage. 'I've seen Mrs Galloway driving Gina round town in that.'

Jas took a deep breath. A problem occurred to her. 'What shall I say if Gina comes and opens the door?'

Liz shrugged. 'Just ask her if she'd like to come round to your house this afternoon. She's bound to say no.'

'Right.' Jas pressed the doorbell. Inside, they heard it ring. There were footsteps, which matched the tempo of Jas's heart, thumping nervously away.

'Hello,' said Mrs Galloway with a smile, recognising Jas. 'If you've come to see Gina, I'm afraid she's out riding with Vale.' Then she began to look a bit uncomfortable. 'Although after all this trouble we've had over that silly fashion show, I'm not sure whether she'd be pleased to see you.'

'You mean because she got caught cheating?' Becky asked cheekily.

Mrs Galloway patted her cream-coloured hair. 'I think perhaps Mr Leach was a little harsh to call

153

it cheating. Some people would call it showing initiative,' she said. But Jas could see that she was embarrassed, all the same.

'I'd call it cheating,' muttered Becky, scuffing her trainers. Mrs Galloway stared at her.

'We didn't come about that,' Jas said cheerfully, taking the packet of cigarettes and the lighter from her pocket. 'I just brought these back for Gina. She left them in my backpack by mistake and I thought she might be needing them.'

Mrs Galloway frowned. 'I don't understand. Gina dosn't smoke.'

Jas put on a perplexed air. 'Are you sure?' Becky and Liz giggled knowingly, precisely on cue. 'Well, I'm certain these are her cigarettes. She told me they were very expensive, so I thought she'd like them back.'

For the first time, Mrs Galloway inspected the packet properly. 'How did she get hold of these?' she asked, looking worried.

'I've no idea.'

'Maybe she showed some initiative,' suggested Becky, holding back a laugh.

Jas smiled politely. 'Anyway, would you give them to her when she gets back from riding?'

Mrs Galloway shook herself. 'Yes, I certainly will. Thank you, Jasmine.' She cast another black look at Becky.

'Bye,' the three of them called as they headed back down the drive.

'Yes!' cried Becky, punching the air as soon as they were out of view of the house. 'I wish I was a fly on the wall so I could see what happens when

Gina gets home. I bet her mum's furious.'

'She won't get anything she doesn't deserve,' said Jas, with feeling. Revenge felt very sweet indeed.

'You're all looking really pleased with yourselves!' Abby came into the sitting room carrying her crash helmet. 'It's nice to see that my little sister's managed to make it up with you,' she told Liz, Charlie and Becky. 'She was a total pain without you guys around to keep her under control.'

'I wasn't!' Jas protested as Abby bent over the chair and tickled her mercilessly.

'Hi, Stuart!' Charlie's face lit up as Stuart came in, looking surprisingly hunky in a leather motorbike jacket.

'Hi, Charlie,' he said cheerfully. 'How's the animal shelter?'

'Okay.' Charlie grinned. 'We're having an open day next month. Maybe you'd like to come down and see what goes on there.'

Stuart nodded. 'I could bring my camera and take some photos. Maybe we could get them in the paper and give you some publicity.'

There was a sound of clinking cans as Abby came in from the kitchen with an armful of Cokes. She handed them out, then squeezed into an armchair with Stuart. 'So, come on, what's happened about Gina and the cigarettes? I've been wondering about it all day.'

'It's wicked!' cried Becky. 'She's been stamping round at school threatening to kill anyone who gets in her way.'

Jas didn't try to hide her delight. 'According to

Vale, after we'd been round, Gina's mum went up to her room and found some cigarette ends. When Gina got home, she was about ready to explode.

'She's been grounded for a month,' Liz revealed. 'She has to go straight home after school.'

'And her mum's halved her allowance,' Charlie added.

'So the poor thing only gets ten pounds a week.' Jas made an ironic sobbing sound. 'But as she's not allowed out, she can't even spend that.'

'That must really hurt!' Abby wiped an imaginary tear from her eye. 'You realise you're going to have to watch your back from now on, Jas. She'll really have the knife out for you in future.'

Jas had thought of that, too. 'I'm keeping well away from her,' she said seriously. 'I've had more than enough of Gina Galloway.'

Abby turned to Stuart. 'How about telling them *your* good news?'

Stuart grinned. 'I had a telephone call from a photographer who does lots of fashion shoots. He'd seen my picture of Jas in the paper and he asked if I'd like to assist him.'

'Wow!' chorused four voices.

Abby held up a finger. 'Wait, it gets better.'

'I told him about you guys, and how you're so interested in fashion and how,' he said, turning to Liz and Charlie and Becky, 'your outfits got ruined before the fashion show. He said that if you'd like to visit his studio for the day, you'll be welcome. Bring your friend Emma, too.'

Jas's jaw dropped. 'We can all go and watch a real fashion shoot?'

156

'Yeah – either that, or he's got a shoot plann[ed] in London in a couple of weeks' time.'

'That's half-term,' Liz calculated. 'We could go to London for the day and maybe go to a concert or see a big show, too.'

Abby smiled. 'And, of course, you'll need an escort – so I could come down with you and watch Stuart assisting.'

'Thanks, Stuart!' Becky was bouncing up and down on the sofa. 'It's a brilliant idea.'

'I thought you deserved something nice,' he said. 'You all seem to have had a pretty tough time recently. You need a treat.'

Abby, who'd been looking across the room towards the window, suddenly got up and stared out. 'What's wrong?' Stuart asked.

'It's nothing.' She shrugged. 'Just that boy on the bike – the one who was riding up and down the road when we drove in. He came past the house again and I saw him looking in.'

'What boy?' Liz went over to Abby and peered out. 'It's Marco Guillano.' She sounded surprised. 'What's he doing here? He lives down by the bakery.'

Jas and Becky shrugged – but Charlie groaned. 'I don't believe it. He must be following me!'

'Why?' Her three friends stared at her with puzzled eyes.

'I said something to him about his dog,' Charlie said with a defiant glance at Liz. 'A couple of times, actually.'

'You shouldn't get involved with him!' Liz said, worried. 'He's really nasty.'

'I know what you told me, Lizzie, but I hate the

157

e treats that dog,' Charlie protested.

/hat's this about his dog?' Abby and Stuart were
.ing puzzled.

He brings his dog to school and makes it do tricks
to show off to the others – and if it doesn't do what
he says, he hits it,' Charlie glowered.

'It isn't just the dog he bashes about.' Jas's chocolate-
coloured eyes were serious. 'He's a bully, Charlie. You
have to be careful.'

Charlie tossed her head. 'Well, he can follow me
round on his bike if he wants, but he can't scare
me . . .'

*Are Charlie's brave words enough to save her from the
school bully? Find out in* Saved by the Bell, *the fifth
book in the Bell Street School series.*

Another Knight Book

Watch out for more books in the Bell Street School series!

MYSTERY BOY
by Holly Tate

Bell Street School 3

Liz Newman is up to something. It all starts when class 2K wins the good conduct prize: a trip to Fantasy World, the great new theme park. But Liz suddenly announces that she may not be going – and she won't say why. Then she starts disappearing after school and telling fibs about what she's been doing, and when Becky, Jas and Charlie ask her what's going on, she starts to avoid them. Is Liz seeing someone? Her friends are determined to find out . . .

MORE GREAT BOOKS AVAILABLE FROM KNIGHT

All these books are available at your local bookshop or newsagent, or can be ordered direct from the publisher. Just tick the titles you want and fill in the form below.

Prices and availability subject to change without notice.

HODDER AND STOUGHTON PAPERBACKS, P.O. Box 11, Falmouth, Cornwall.

Please send cheque or postal order for the value of the book, and add the following for postage and packing.

U.K. – 80p for one book, and 20p for each additional book ordered up to a £2.00 maximum.

B.F.P.O. – 80p for the first book, and 20p for each additional book.

OVERSEAS INCLUDING EIRE – £1.50 for the first book, plus £1.00 for the second book, and 30p for each additional book ordered.

OR Please debit this amount from my Access/Visa Card (delete as appropriate).

Card Number

AMOUNT £ ....

EXPIRY DATE ....

SIGNED ....

NAME ....

ADDRESS ....